Unique-Visual Narratives

Asya Sakine Uçar

Unique-Visual Narratives

The Evolution of Art and Literature in Turkey

PETER LANG

Berlin - Bruxelles - Chennai - Lausanne - New York - Oxford

Library of Congress Cataloging-in-Publication Data
A CIP catalog record for this book has been applied for at the Library of Congress.

Names: Uçar, Asya Sakine, 1987- author.
Title: Unique - visual narratives : the evolution of art and literature in
    Turkey / Asya Sakine Uçar.
Description: New York : Peter Lang, 2025. | Series: Tartu historical
    studies, 2191-0480 ; vol. 8 | Includes bibliographical references.
Identifiers: LCCN 2024052775 (print) | LCCN 2024052776 (ebook) | ISBN
    9783631919149 (paperback) | ISBN 9783631931356 (pdf) | ISBN
    9783631931363 (epub)
Subjects: LCSH: Gülsoy, Murat, 1967- Ressam Vasıf'ın gizli aşklar tarihi.
    | Vassaf, Gündüz. Ressamın isyanı. | Art in literature. | Art and
    literature--Turkey. | LCGFT: Literary criticism.
Classification: LCC PL248.G743 R47383 2025 (print) | LCC PL248.G743
    (ebook) | DDC 894/.3534--dc23/eng/20241214
LC record available at https://lccn.loc.gov/2024052775
LC ebook record available at https://lccn.loc.gov/2024052776

Bibliographic Information published by the Deutsche Nationalbibliothek
The Deutsche Nationalbibliothek lists this publication in the Deutsche Nationalbibliografie;
detailed bibliographic data is available in the internet at http://dnb.d-nb.de.

Cover Image: Early cave drawing and shamanism figures
© Asya Sakine Uçar

ISSN: 2191-0480
ISBN: 978-3-631-91914-9 (Print)
E-ISBN: 978-3-631-93135-6 (E-PDF)
E-ISBN: 978-3-631-93136-3 (E-PUB)
DOI: 10.3726/ b22594

© 2025 Peter Lang Group AG, Lausanne
Published by Peter Lang GmbH, Berlin, Germany

info@peterlang.com - www.peterlang.com

Table of Contents

Foreword

Thanks to my enthusiasm for art and painting in particular, I have taken on many journeys, both imaginatively and literally. I hope this book becomes a testament not only to my passion but it also inspires readers to embark on their own journeys while discovering the intricate connections between visual arts and literature in Turkish context. I now realize that as the years go by, we grow older, see more, read more, travel more, but the most precious peace and happiness is found when you retreat into your own shell and become smaller. I believe in hard times we need a narrative to hold onto, and I found mine in our "village house" that gave me the space to translate my painting skills from canvases to walls and even to pots I found in the trash. In full recognition of how life is short and art is long, I would like to dedicate this book to my dear mother and beloved late father as in his valuable memory I wish to keep my promise and make a painting "Highland" depicting the changing aspects of the seasons…

May 25, 2024

Notes for the Reader

Unless, otherwise stated, the translations from Turkish sources including the novels belong to me. As art and literature have been two parallel themes steering my academic studies, just as exciting as writing the book was designing the cover picture which is largely inspired by shamanism and early cave paintings as a token of my gratitude to the origins of art itself.

"The feeling of being one! That is the essence of art. The interesting thing is that, that is also the essence of being human. To be unique, to be like no other." (Gülsoy 86)

Introduction

The seeds of writing this book were planted when I consecutively read two fascinating novels; Murat Gülsoy's *Painter Vasıf's History of Secret Loves* and Gündüz Vassaf's *Painter's Rebellion*, both published in 2023. The idea of building a connection between art and literature with a focus on contemporary Turkish novels that predominantly feature art, paintings, and painters has its deep roots both in a strong desire to engage creatively with visual arts and take my literary awareness a step further after studying the correlation between visual arts and verbal representations, ekphrasis in A. S. Byatt's *The Frederica Quartet* in my Ph.D. dissertation in 2019. With this study, I want to take a different perspective and show visual narratives are not merely limited with the situation that an artwork inspires a textual work but the transfer of images from the writers to the readers and visual thinking perform major parts in creative writing. This study enlightens the experiences of composing novels about visual arts and the ways in which this was impacted not only by creative imagination and the skill of the writer but also personal practices and modern narrative tools which could be a pivotal universal aspect for the book.

Images, which constitute the initial spark of artistic creation are composed of a combination of events and phenomena that come to life in the artist's mind as he/she perceives the external and internal world through his/her own perception filter, a unique lens through which the artist interprets and processes stimuli contributing to the artistic expression. These images can take on both visual and literary form suggesting a duality in transferring the mental imagery but allowing a rich interplay for both modes of expression. As in all branches of art, the effects of poetry and painting on the listener/reader and the viewer and the impressions they create can manifest in many different forms. Throughout the history of art, we see these effects sometimes arising from the presentation of poetry in a visual format and other times from the expression of painting through poetic language. Visual narratives are composed of a perceiving-visualizing-re-presenting process which provides a territory of investigation where insights into how artists paint and how writers write, become amplified and potentially accessible (Krauth and Bowman 12). Rather than merely depicting a picture or an image within a painting, in the chosen novels both authors craft comprehensive narrative structures that weave visual images into aesthetic forms that distinguishes their works as primary examples of innovative novel forms. Eventually, what the novelists create as character and action is predominantly inspired by art, artists or artworks and provides essential elaboration for historical and cultural authenticity.

The design of the book is based on a structure consisting of three main parts with subtitles and an introduction. The first part aims to display how the connection between visual representations, which have been in a constant relationship of continuity and change throughout the centuries, has been the subject of both philosophy and art, from ancient cave drawings with shamanistic rituals at its core, to contemporary art critics, and has been analyzed from many different perspectives. The enduring fascination with the interplay between writing and painting encapsulates the foundational and integral role of painting in early human history hinging upon the convergence of visual representation and verbal narrative. The first part comprises art and literature scene in Turkey examining the historical background, how the tradition of painting, art is also interconnected with first written accounts in Turkish literary records and how cultural transitions, most importantly diverse religious beliefs impacted the artistic domains. Ottoman miniature art, its pioneering and pivotal aspect of illustrative narrative style, Orhan Pamuk's re-imagination of miniatures and the artists in his historical novel *My Name is Red* evidence how word and image are intertwined creating a hybridity in the form of a combination where western narrative structure and the art of the East/Islam meet. In evoking the kinship between words and images, and how the art of writing involves conjuring images with words, Pamuk's *The Naive and Sentimental Novelist* sets a paradigm with great relevance to the analysis of the novels as Pamuk emphasizes how the writer's visual imagination and painterly allusions shape the narrative. The transition to modern European trends in art, aesthetics, ideas and movements which initiated a tradition of poetry-painting fusion led by notable artists like Nazım Hikmet, Tevfik Fikret and Bedri Rahmi Eyüboğlu is elucidated in the subsection "Poet-painters in Turkish Literature." The first part of the book establishes a vanguard and illuminating connection with the novels as apart from the pivotal role of art in both novels, the backbone of Murat Gülsoy's novel is the historical transformation of Turkey and how modern painting was born and developed and Gündüz Vassaf's novel lays a bridge between the inquisition and the totalitarian systems of Caravaggio's time and its analogies with certain figures from Turkish history and also what the narrating character/author has been through personally.

Part II aims to give a detailed analysis of Gülsoy's *Painter Vasıf's History of Secret Loves* augmenting how the power of the pictures inspire writing which is already a special field of interest for the author who has been organizing seminars, workshops on creative writing at various institutions. Gülsoy, distinctively creates a painter character who is based on a fusion of fiction, as he is transfigured through the writer's imagination and the real given the time period he is born into and the figures he is associated with. Gülsoy conceptualizes his documentary novel as a tribute to those who founded and developed modern art of painting in Turkey which explains the inclusion of so many real, historical figures (some of them are the poet-painters to be discussed in the first part) in the novel intertwining the reality and fiction at some points. Vasıf's lifetime encapsulates the dynamic changes and evolving artistic practices especially for the art of painting in the transformative eras of the country which correspond to the last period of Ottoman Empire and the foundation of the republic. There are several subtitles articulated in this part which include discussions on the role of creative writing in intersecting visual arts with literature and blending history with fiction. It is also possible to examine and explore the character's background, personal relationships in a historical and cultural context which culminate in the sections elaborating the political art scene in reference to "Group D Painters" and the representation and place of women in artistic practices. Moreover, the inter-genre of the novel gains another dimension with the help of artificial intelligence programs as Gülsoy uses one in order to create the picture on the cover, the rotating pictures in the novel's promotional video and the retrospective booklet, which compiles examples of Vasıf's paintings and drawings throughout his life.

Part III, which focuses on Gündüz Vassaf's *Painter's Rebellion*, tells the search and love story of an unnamed character who becomes enchanted after seeing Italian painter Caravaggio's painting *Burial of Saint Lucy* which is located in a church in Syracuse, Sicily. The aim of this part is to illustrate how this particular painting becomes the point of reference or visual stimuli for the character who embarks on a long journey of self-discovery through the story of Caravaggio, his life and artworks. In the meantime, the defining characteristics of Caravaggio's art like the dramatic contrast between dark and light, called *chiaroscuro* resonates with the extremes of his life as using a single light source like a candle to illuminate the characters or casting deep shadows not only heightens the contrast but also the drama which is reverberant of the artist's rebellious nature and turbulent life pervaded by murder, exile and imprisonment. The narrating character/author who is obsessed with Caravaggio, is actually tracing his own life through his paintings, passionately trying to unravel the mystery of his death. Such that the wonder and introspection becomes an impetus for Vassaf/the narrator to verbalize his highly visual journey which proceeds in accordance with Caravaggio's own journey from Rome, Naples, Malta to Sicily, and meditates his experiences in the form of a novel as it becomes a vehicle of visual storytelling. Once again in different subtitles, this part delineates Caravaggio's tumultuous life and personality, his unconventional approach to art alluding to major works from his oeuvre especially with a focus on the themes of death, decapitation and violence revealing his own fears and anxieties. Documenting the character's museum visits to major European cities like Paris, London, Florence and Rome, art and history are seamlessly interwoven into the narrative ensuring a comprehensive study of Caravaggio's legacy. Gündüz Vassaf also provides QR code of the Wiki Art encyclopedia for the Caravaggio paintings, creates a music selection on Spotify for the music he references in the book and another QR access to a petition for vindication of Giordano Bruno who was burned alive because of his unorthodox beliefs in sixteenth century Rome.

The conclusion part consolidates how the novels obviously relate to each other, in particular in their shared fascination with the visual arts. Life and art is merged in such a profound and fictional framework in these novels that ultimately they become indiscernible as the borders between fact and fiction, reality and imagination are demolished. The intersection of verbal and visual representations enables intellectual, emotional and even sensory participation for readers as composing novels about visual arts suggests an exploration of a specific form of writing. Apart from imagination in bringing visual elements to life in written words, AI-generated contents or other technological interventions also impact creative writing process and implies a deeper understanding of the interaction between visual and written forms. With this book, as far as Turkish art and literature scene is concerned, I intend to draw attention to articulating inspiratory and guiding aspects of art in augmenting writing skills in the form of novel as visual narratives extend beyond the inspiration of artwork and the verbalization of visual journeys is an effective tool of storytelling within a historical, cultural, and artistic context.

Chapter 1
Art and Literature in Turkey

Historical Roots of Art

Our knowledge of human history begins with painting. Drawings made on cave walls at a time when history was not yet recorded in writing give us the first clues about the lives of primitive people. In these first linguistic indicators, writing and painting are almost indistinguishable from one another. These first drawings/paintings, which would later form the core of the alphabet, prove that writing and painting have been intertwined since the beginning of history. The connection between these visual representations, which have been in a constant relationship of continuity and change throughout the following centuries, has been the subject of both philosophy and art, from ancient Greek philosophers to contemporary art critics, and has been analyzed from many different perspectives. The enduring fascination with the interplay between writing and painting encapsulates the foundational and integral role of painting in early human history hinging upon the convergence of visual representation and verbal narrative.

Long held is the idea that, in the history of art, there is interaction between literature, music, cinema, painting, architecture, sculpture and other branches of art as what shapes the artist's creative endeavors is drawing inspiration from everything around. The relationship between visual arts and literature has brought different approaches throughout the ages with deep historical roots. The affinity between painting and literature or writing and the history of book illustration dates back to the first miniature manuscripts in China, Central Asia and Egypt in the second century BC continuing across civilizations for centuries including Greece, Rome, Europe, Seljuks and Ottomans. What is essential for a work of art is the image and the criteria of subjectivity as the images aroused in the minds is different although the external world is thought to be the same for everyone. According to Gombrich, this is a transposition rather than a copy: "For the artist, too, cannot transcribe what he sees; he can only translate it into the terms of his medium. He, too, is strictly tied to the range of tones which his medium will yield" (36). Burnett sees it as "visualization" which is an important distinction as "visualization is about the relationship between images and human creativity" (14). When an image is transformed into a work of art and presented to viewers, it enters a dynamic process of interpretation, perception and reproduction. The diversity of interpretation, artistic dialog and the adventure of the image recreated, is in a continuous cycle of interaction between the artist and the readers, listeners or viewers.

The history of 'writing' which was invented because of the need to perpetuate 'word' to resist historical process, dates back to petroglyphs, paintings carved on rocks and stones. As the pictorial symbolic conceptions that are traced in petroglyphs simplify, they are

> reduced into geometric forms, as these forms are symbolized by repetition, they consti-
> tute the first examples of writing. Therefore, although today visual images and writing
> are kept completely separate from each other, the process of the formation of writing
> was based on images. (Ekici 55)

Painting, which developed after the figures drawn on cave walls and eventually turned into an art form, has played an important role in the expression of human emotions and dreams. In his seminal work *The Story of Art*, Gombrich remarks that "it is much more likely that these are the oldest relics of that universal beef in the power of picture-making…" (63). In the art of painting, which started with imitating nature, it was accepted as a primary goal to reveal the likeness of what was depicted.

When it comes to human creativity and imagination, cave art, often linked to the origins of shamanism, seems to represent the earliest visual narratives. As an ancient belief and practice system, and having existed in different parts of the world from North America to Asia, shamanism has both a spiritual and practical involvement with nature, healing, magic and transformation as the shamans[1] are believed to have interacts and communications with the spiritual world experiencing altered states of consciousness. The confluence between shamanism and cave paintings as the first visual manifestations is a debated yet widely accepted theory as it is possible to treat shamanism as the archetype of art. This affinity also shapes the understanding of Upper Paleolithic cave art, especially those found in France (Lascaux and Chauvet) and Spain (Altamira) and shamanic rituals, transcendental and mystical visions that are trajected into the symbolic signs and images on the cave walls.[2] It is possible to apply the intuition and meditation that one finds in artistic process and creation to the ecstasy and spiritual catharsis that is associated with shamanistic rituals. It is also evident that Turks

---

1   In her book *Shamanism: An Introduction*, Margaret Stutley writes that the origin of the term shaman (the ecstatic one) is still disputed but among the views put forward are Tungus word *s'aman*, Pali term samana (Sanskrit *s'ramana*) and the Chinese *sha-men*. She also adds that shaman could be a Tungus term belonging to the Turko-Mongolian language and the Turkic-speaking people use the term *kam*. (3)

2   Susan Michaelson outlines in her work "The Hand on the Wall of the Cave. Exploring Connections Between Shamanism and the Visual Arts" that "French pre-historian, Jean Clottes, in his book Les Chamanes de la Préhistoire, co-written with David Lewis-Williams, has drawn on both anthropology and neuroscience to suggest that the images on the walls of the caves at Pech Merle and also at Lascaux, were created by artists who were also shamans and that they may have been created as part of some sort of ritual involving trance or altered states of consciousness." (293)

are familiar with shamanism and even after converting to Islam, certain elements have been syncretized into the newly adopted religious practices. Deriving from the fact that the universe is divided into three parts; sky, earth and underground and the Sky God is believed to be the one and only deity, in his work "Turkish and Mongol Shamanism in the Middle Ages" John Andrew Boyle argues that depending on the abilities like foretelling the future or curing diseases, doctor, magician, wizard all denote shaman and his chief characteristic is going into a trance during which the soul leaves the body and ascends to the sky and descends to the underworld (178). On a further note, *qam* (Turkish word for shaman) is also referred to in Mahmud al-Kashgari's Turkish-Arabic lexicon in the second half of the eleventh century as equivalent to *kahin* which means foreteller (178). The aesthetic analysis of art and architecture in the Hun, Gokturk and Uighur States also disclose the existence of shamanism that is mostly found in animistic depictions.

The literary tradition of Turkish culture can be traced to the Orkhun Valley in Mongolia as The Gokturks erected monuments in the 720s and 730s giving narrative accounts of their experiences hence composing the earliest example of Turkish literature. Of those monuments, while the Kül Tigin monument was erected by his older brother Bilge Kagan in 732, the Bilge Kagan monument was erected by his own son, in 735, one year after his death. It is believed that the Tonyukuk monument was erected by himself in 720–725 (Ergin 6). It is diffi-cult to know when the first artistic creations of the Turks emerged. Since there is no concrete data on the exact origins of early periods historically, the first documents of the Turks can be dated back to the seventh century. The Choyr/Choyren Inscription, which is thought to date back to 687 AD and consists of a stone in the shape of a human body, is known to be the oldest record—for the time being—with various shapes resembling writing and painting on it (Ercivan, Kabakçı and Köseoğlu 294). However, as the research to interpret the inscrip-tions on it continues, the Gokturk Inscriptions (Orkhun Monuments) are still accepted as the oldest written documents of the Turkic language. As Talat Tekin mentions in his book, the Orkhon inscriptions are not merely a history of warfare in which political and military events are described in the order of their occur-rence, but they also present the oldest and most beautiful examples of oratory in Turkish language (15). The following words on the monuments erected with the alphabet known as runic script, which consists of letters suitable for writing on hard objects such as stone, marble, etc., are remarkable: "…I sent for painters and sculptors from the Chinese Khan…. […] I had them build a marvelous shrine and put splendid paintings and sculptures inside (and) outside." (trans. from Tekin, 39). The word bedizçi "painter" in the Gokturk Inscriptions indicates that the Turks had a tradition of painting, or at least an interest in painting and the debut of poetry in the Uighurs, probably in the sixth century has initiated a continuous and vibrant tradition.

Spanning the histories of tribal communities, major states and empires like the Seljuk and the Ottoman, Turkish literature encapsulates a diverse range of creative endeavors with a dynamic nature in conformity with the changing aspects of political, cultural, and economic environments. Through the centuries, from the nomadic existence to the formation of large states across Asia to the vast Ottoman Empire which lasted from the thirteenth to early twentieth centuries and finally modern Turkish Republic, the Turkish communities are characterized by an interplay of religious and linguistic influences. For that reason, it is important to note that the history of Turkish painting projects diverse religious beliefs and cultural transitions that shaped the artistic domains over the centuries. The Turks have been active in the field of painting within the framework of three religions; namely Manichaeism, Buddhism and Islam. In the Uighurs, who adopted Manichaeism and later Buddhism between seventh and ninth centuries A.D., the art of painting, as a result of these two religious views and understandings, manifested itself in the form of wall and ceiling paintings, especially in temples and monasteries. Actually, Old Uighur Turks played significant role in the development of poetry and painting as they had a rich cultural and artistic tradition; their contributions laid the groundwork for the flourishing of arts in the following ages. According to Biçer, the most important data on Uighur culture are obtained thanks to the archaeological excavations in the Turfan Basin that continued from the last quarter of the nineteenth century to the first quarter of the twentieth century (126). The wall paintings unearthed during these excavations contain influences from Chinese, Indian and Greek art showcasing the intercultural interaction. In the tenth century, the adoption of Islam marked a significant change challenging the continuation of traditional painting forms and representational art. The art of painting began to lose its power due to the new religion's prohibition of painting and distinctive forms like calligraphy, geometric patterns were developed as a response to the restrictions.

From the thirteenth century onwards, the tradition of Turkish painting persisted in various forms combining writing with painting in unique ways marking Turkish-Islamic painting. The art of calligraphy, which began to develop in this period, emerges as the only art in which painting and writing are seamlessly integrated into a whole. In addition to calligraphy, which continued in the Ottoman period, Divan poetry also offers a unique structure that combines poetry and painting in a single frame due to the poetic expressions called *mazmuns* it contains. Such a synthesis can be found in texts like the Oghuz Khan Epic[3] or the Dede Korkut[4] Tales in that some of the heroes are depicted in such detail that these parts of the texts turn into vivid paintings. The epic and lyric tradition recounting heroic exploits has generated foundational texts of Turkish oral tradition representing seminal aspects of folk tales, legends and stories. In *A Millennium of Turkish Literature* Talat Halman writes:

> Among the oldest specimens of written literary works are memorial tablets, stone monoliths, and stelae found in the Yenisei Valley of north-eastern Mongolia as well as documents unearthed in the Sinkiang region of modern China. Dating from the seventh to the ninth century, these works include stories of the battles the Turks fought against the Chinese, a variety of legends, and numerous specimens of verse (found mostly in Chinese translation) written in Uyghur Turkish. (6)

The intersection of the words and images or how the power of the words evoke images has evolved in Turkish literature as well through ekphrastic experiences that could be traced in Evliya Çelebi's *Seyahatname*, a ten-volume travel book written in Ottoman Turkish between 1673 and 1685 in Cairo, where he spent the last years of his life. Evliyâ Çelebi's *Seyahatnâme*, endeavors to provide his readers with topographical, geographical, folkloric, architectural, cultural, artistic, ethnological, etymological, historical and political information about the places he visited. Apart from paintings and sculptures, it is possible to find detailed depictions of architectural works, wall and tomb inscriptions. Nilay Kaya draws attention to the fact that Çelebi first gives objective information about the buildings; their structural features, locations and dimensions before making personal evaluations about the aesthetic characteristics of the buildings. As the narrative progresses, the dimensions of subjectivity increase and psychological, sociological, political, religious, cultural and similar factors come into play (240). Finally, the art of miniature painting, which gained great prominence in the Ottoman Empire, not only decorated poetry books intricately interweaving poetry with the painting, merging the visual with the literary, but it also continued the art of painting in a more secular context.

---

3   "It is an elaborate and lyrical description of superhuman and worldly episodes in the life of the legendary hero Oğuz." (Halman 6)

4   "*The Book of Dede Korkut*, composed of twelve legends, narrates in prose and verse the adventures of the Oğuz Turks migrating from Central Asia to Asia Minor. These tales of heroism constitute the Turks' principal national epic, which invites comparison with the world's best epic literature." (Halman 8)

The Art of Painting-Ottoman Miniature Art

The word "miniature" comes from the word "miniatura," which refers to ornamentation made in red color (as the word "miniare" means to paint with red) around the calligraphic letters at the beginning of sections in medieval Europe manuscripts. However, over time, with the influence of the word minor (small), it began to be used for very finely crafted small-sized paintings. In Islamic art, miniature was called depiction and the miniature artist was called *musavvir* or *nakkaş*. Among the characteristics of the miniature painting is that techniques such as perspective, anatomy, light and shadow are not employed. As an important artistic heritage in Islamic culture, miniature with its own distinctive style emphasizes detailed ornamentation, decorative function enhancing the aesthetic appeal and narrative illustration depicting scenes from history, literature, palace, battles or daily life.

When it comes to the techniques and characteristics of miniature art, the absence of depth, perspective, light, and shadow stand out as opposed to the western art. As color is the element that appeals to the senses most in miniature, it is important to choose bright and vivid colors like red which is the most prominent color in distribution. In general, while red is preferred on the figures and architecture, blues are used for the sky and ground. Miniature works are first drawn as sketches and then transferred onto paper and polished with gold. Living beings and objects are abstracted from nature and transformed into decorative elements that significantly differ from their real appearance. The human figure, which turns into a two-dimensional mold as in the shadow play, is disproportionate to the objects around it. One of the most interesting features of miniature art is that the height increases according to the importance of the person, and the person to be emphasized is strategically placed in the foreground and emphasized with a long stature.

Miniature art developed under Ottoman patronage and became the original Ottoman miniature art in the period from Mehmet II to Suleyman I. As outlined by Özden Fırat, "miniature painting or *taswir* and *nakish,* as the Ottomans called it—was the dominant form of pictorial art until the eighteenth century" (26) and "it developed together with medieval Islamic book illustration—alongside illumination (tezhip), calligraphy (hat), paper marbling (ebru), and bookbinding (cilt)" (26–27). Miniature art was used in the Ottoman period to depict sultans' pictures, wars and historical events shedding light on the present day as historical documents. Among the main miniaturized manuscripts produced during this period, which is also important in terms of the history of Ottoman miniature art, are *Hünername, Surname-i Hümayun,* and *Şahname-i Selim Khan,* which depict the daily lives of the Ottoman sultans, festivities and victories.

> Miniature is like a vivid translation of story, poetry and history. When you look at a miniature, you see how the artist who created that work has brought the philosophy of life, the morality, the customs and traditions, the dressing styles of the period and the historical events of the society he grew up in to the present day. (Binark 278)

In that sense, Ottoman miniature art not only served as a form of artistic expression but also played a crucial role in documenting historical and cultural aspects of the Ottoman society with its ability in capturing the essence of life, morals and traditions.

Miniatures from fifteenth and early sixteenth centuries are devoid of a unified, unique visual language as the influence of Venetian artists like Bellini and the grapples of local artists are obvious. In representing the early Ottoman miniature style in Turkish miniature art, important developments took place during the reign of Mehmed the Conqueror (1432–1481). The portrait of Mehmed the Conqueror made by Gentile Bellini (1429–1507), who was invited from Italy after the conquest of Istanbul, and the bronze medallions by Costanzo da Ferrara (1429–1507) highly influenced the artistic styles of the Ottoman painters like Sinan Bey and Şiblîzâde Ahmed whose portraits of the Conqueror are reminiscent of the miniature tradition. For that reason, "the oil portraiture of the West was transformed into miniature portraiture in the hands of nakkaş" (Koç 170) which paved the way for the transition to the art of painting in the Western sense or it would not be wrong to speculate that a cultural relationship in the East-West sense first began with Mehmed the Conqueror.

The political and cultural contacts established with the Italian states during the reign of Mehmed II, the geographical location of Istanbul connecting continents and seas, and the policies of the sultan blended Eastern culture with Western culture, paving the way for new syntheses in the interaction of Eastern and Western forms of art. Produced by Italian artists at the request of Mehmed II, the paintings and medallions link Turkish art to Western art as the first objects of diplomatic and cultural exchange in the field of art, while also offering a documentary quality as a symbol of intercultural dialog. Bellini's portrait of Mehmed the Conqueror is a realistic and detailed depiction of the sultan outside the miniature tradition and is considered the first naturalistic portrait of an Ottoman sultan in the West. This particular portrait evidences the fact that "Mehmet II was the only Muslim ruler of his time to adopt a western pictorial language" (Necipoğlu 264) which not only meant fostering cultural exchange between the Ottoman Empire and the Italian Renaissance as an extension of diplomacy but also commissioning elaborate works of art allowed promising channels of artistic transfer. In his pursuit of the portrait, Elizabeth Rodini attributes an iconic status for Bellini's painting in the sense that it is "a vehicle for thinking about relationships, between artist and subject and among those who came later, including scholars, collectors, institutions, and even nations" (8).

During the reign of Suleyman the Magnificent (1494–1566), Ottoman miniature painting passed through important stages and moved towards its original style, and the subjects of Turkish miniatures developed in the form of historical events, war scenes, palace life, equestrian play, hunting scenes and portraits. Matrakçı Nasuh (1480–1564) was one of the most important painters of the period with his landscapes and topographical city views; with a realistic approach he depicted the cities, castles, rivers, countryside, seas and harbors that were crossed during the expeditions. Nakkaş Osman, the chief miniaturist of the period was another leading miniaturist while the Ottoman navy and naval battles were the central topics in the manuscripts.

During the reign of Sultan Ahmed III (1673–1736), who was a master calligrapher, there was a great progress in painting and miniature art as in other branches of art. Levnî Abdülcelil Çelebi (?–1732), the famous painter of this period, is a personality who left deep traces in Ottoman culture with his new orientations and influenced the visual art of the period. Günsel Renda mentions how Levni's miniatures of the poet Vehbi's *Surname* depicting the festivities of the circumcision of Ahmed III's four sons, male and female figures and even the portraits of sultans are important in bringing a new perception of depth to the art of miniature (402). Levnî's paintings, which preserve the values of traditional miniature art while introducing innovations, reflect this new phase in Ottoman painting. The scholarly researches on miniatures forge how these works are valuable in pertaining to the present corpus going beyond art-historical context, reifying their eras and exerting their agency to the present with versatile modes of thinking on art and the visual culture.

After the eighteenth century, Ottoman painting saw a shift from book illustration to new branches such as hand-drawn wall paintings. This led to the decoration of palaces, mansions, fountains, and even the walls of mosques and tombs. During this period, the development of diplomatic and commercial relations brought many European painters to the Ottoman capital. These artists, known as the "Bosphorus Painters," became renowned for their Istanbul landscapes. The concept of Western painting was first introduced at the educational level in the Mühendishane-i Berr-i Hümayun, established in 1793. Painting lessons were initially included in military schools and later in civilian schools. Landscape painters who graduated from these institutions became the first representatives of Western-style painting in the Ottoman Empire. In 1883, the Sanayi-i Nefise School was founded, modeled after the Fine Arts Academies in the West. The military painters who laid the foundations of Turkish painting helped spread painting education, significantly increasing interest in art. Detailed information about military painters and subsequently formed groups like D painters will be given in the second part within the analysis of Murat Gülsoy's novel.

At the beginning of the nineteenth century, portraits and paintings of the sultans began to be painted in different styles, and miniatures were generally replaced by oil paintings. The artists of this period made an effort to reinterpret Western influences in their works without breaking away from traditions, and they became the pioneers of the new painting tradition with educational enterprises initiated in the schools opened after the Tanzimat. In the eighteenth century, the urge to adapt to the changing technological and geopolitical developments marked a significant period of transformation and modernization in the Ottoman Empire. Embarking on a series of reforms, most notably Tanzimat reforms in the mid-nineteenth century not only meant westernization movement, but it also had profound impact on various aspects of life including the arts. Ottoman Westernization emerged as a simultaneous symptom of the state's military decline after 1683 and as a trend that anticipated the more decisive modernization reforms of the nineteenth century (Koç 186). The gradual weakening of The Ottoman Empire coinciding with the increasing political, economic, and technological power of Europe wielded an influence as from the eighteenth century onwards the Ottomans commenced new ideas and institutions as "Turkish intellectuals started seeking the empire's salvation in technological development, political reform, and cultural progress fashioned after European prototypes" (Halman 63).

Beginning in 1835, talented students were sent to European capitals like Vienna, Berlin, Paris and London to study painting. However, Mekteb-i Osmani was opened in 1861 in Paris, in order to provide better education for students and it later became the center for these studies. The aim of this practice was not only to provide these young people with a better education, but also to help them acquire a "Western identity" as high-level members of the future Ottoman society. Osman Hamdi Bey, in particular, is recognized as a pioneer of painting and his groundbreaking contributions as an archeologist. Most notably known for his *The Tortoise Trainer* (1906), Osman Hamdi embraced Western techniques while incorporating elements from Turkish and Islamic culture giving rise to his paintings being seen as the internalization of the Western view of the East by an Easterner.

The transition to European art trends and the emergence of new forms aligning with modern aesthetics caused a decline in the art of miniature and eventual closure of *nakkashanes*, the traditional workshops miniature artists worked. As the nineteenth century witnessed an exposure to Western ideas and movements for Ottoman intellectuals, the tradition of visual arts-poetry or painting-poetry gained a different dimension. From the nineteenth century onwards, in alliance with changing cultural landscape artists shifted to a more modern line being influenced by various Western movements in both poetry and painting. Poets were the principal conveyers of the modernization and the relevant reforms, and they showed strenuous effort to adhere to the classical folk conventions and at the same time experiment with the tastes of the West.

Poet-Painters in Turkish Literature

It is also possible to find artists who have ventured beyond different mediums of expressions as some poets are equally drawn to projecting their ideas in visual forms in Turkish literature. Artists with a command of the visual and literary arts can choose the creative medium that best expresses their ideas. Simonides of Ceos's famous remark "painting is mute poetry, poetry speaking picture" elucidates verbal transformations of pictorial sources or the visual manifestations of literary sources. The profound connection between poetry and painting has already been recognized and introspected with poignant figures like William Wordsworth (1770–1850) and William Blake (1757–1827) who elucidated how pictorial manifestations and verbal transformations interact with each other. To begin with, one of the most notable multifaceted artists, William Blake was a poet, painter and engraver in that his poems and paintings invite to a dreamlike and supernatural world integrating his poetic discourse with visual elements. The dynamic pairing of poetry and painting also remind of Pre-Raphaelite Brotherhood, founded in 1849 by a group of friends, artists, poets like William Holman Hunt, Dante Gabriel Rossetti, John Everett Millais and Christina Rossetti who were integral in shaping the themes and aesthetic principles of the movement. For example, in Özlem Uzundemir's book titled *İmgeyi Konuşturmak: İngiliz Yazınında Görsel Sanatlar*, in which she analyzes examples of ekphrasis in English poetry and fiction from the Romantic period to the twentieth century, she quotes that Pre-Raphaelites hope to end the clash between poetry and painting alleging that every picture has a narrative (65). The Pre-Raphaelite painters, who formed a union in England, reflected nature with a poetic atmosphere suggesting the emotive and narrative qualities that can be conveyed through visual arts. Such specific examples illustrating the direct impact of visual art on poetic forms underscore how poetry in pictorial forms or painting in poetic language can enrich the creative output. Accordingly, such deep appreciation for the interconnectedness of various arts is epitomized largely by poet-painters in Turkish literature as we have many artists who express themselves in these two fields. Starting from Tevfik Fikret (1867–1915), Nazım Hikmet (1902–1963), Bedri Rahmi Eyüboğlu (1911–1975), Abidin Dino (1913–1993), İlhan Berk (1918–2008), Oktay Rıfat (1814–1988), Metin Eloğlu (1927–1985), Cemal Süreya (1931–1990), Fikri Cantürk (1933–2019), Komet (1941–2022), Ekrem Kahraman (b.1948), Bünyamin Balamir (b.1953) and many others exemplify the interdisciplinary nature of artistic expression and the ways in which poetry and visual arts intersect in Turkish literature and culture.

Towards the end of the nineteenth century, Tevfik Fikret was the most important representative of a literary movement that emerged as a continuation of the second generation of Tanzimat in the renewal line of Turkish literature that was formed around the journal Servet-i Fünûn, from which it took its name. As a member of the journal, Fikret became part of a cultural milieu that highlighted visual arts; in fact, prints were made from pictures in European magazines, accompanied by poems written underneath. The publication of photographs and paintings in Turkish journals, which gradually increased in number and developed after Tanzimat, gave rise to the trend of writing poetry under painting. In Turkish literature, this trend of writing poems under pictures, paintings or photographs, describing their subjects in poetry by looking at the pictures and making them speak started in 1882 in the journal Mir'ât-ı Âlem. Tevfik Fikret was also among those who wrote poems under paintings, and sometimes even painted the pictures himself. According to Cahit Kavcar it is possible to evaluate Fikret's liaison with painting from three different perspectives; namely he is a painter himself, writes poems under his paintings, and paints through poetry (137). In some of his poems, Fikret employs techniques intrinsic to painting, organizing the verses with a perspective that mirrored visual arts. In his final years, Fikret retreated to his own house in Rumelihisarı which is a dwelling named Aşiyan and serves as a museum today preserving his indelible legacy. In this house, not only in poetry but in various artistic pursuits including painting, Fikret immerses himself. For instance, in his poem entitled "While Painting," he imagines and articulates the distress and nuisance of creation process as the poem is about an artist in the act of painting.

Drawing attention to the combination of painting and poetry in newspapers and magazines rather than in books, Seval Şahin mentions that Servet-i Fünun poets had a great share in this, and that their reflection of nature in their poems as if they were painters brought them closer to the principles of parnassism (139).

Thus, like many of his peers, Tevfik Fikret is also thought to be under the influence of parnassism. In her book on French poetry, Maria Rubins defines that "'Parnasse' refers to a group of poets who published their verse in *Le Parnasse contemporain*" (31) in the nineteenth century, "synthesiz[ing] various artistic media, particularly the verbal and plastic" (41). Moreover, although many of those poets "called for a union of all the arts, it was the visual arts they valued most…" (53). The Parnassians have origins in the romantics in their embrace of fusing different forms of artistic mediums bridging the gap between the verbal and the visual. Accordingly, Fikret also sees painting and poetry akin to each other, hence composing or organizing his poems seeking the same principles reminiscent of painting. The Parnassians' faithful reflection of nature, capturing all its intricate details aligns with descriptive poetry tradition and correlatively Fikret, in his nature poems, utilizes adjectives to add a painterly quality and precision to his works. His poem "Traces" and the painting *Autumn* exemplify this parallel approach as in the poem Fikret describes the path he takes from his home (Aşiyan) to Robert College, where he works, conveying the difficulties of life through vivid imagery. Similarly, in the painting "Autumn," he depicts this path in all its detailed splendor, thus bridging the gap between poetry and painting by portraying the same scene through two different artistic mediums.

Nazım Hikmet, who lived between 1901 and 1963, is one of the artists who was also interested in painting, although he is mostly known for his literary identity. Nazım Hikmet's interest in painting is thought to have started thanks to his mother Celile Hanım, who was also a painter. Hikmet harbored his keen interest in painting during his time in prison where he produced many works encompassing portraits of himself, his friends and depictions of prison life. Notably, Hikmet wrote poems inspired by the paintings of Turkish artists, like İbrahim Balaban, whom he knew intimately from his prison days. Three ekphrastic poems by Hikmet dedicated to Balaban's paintings are prominent as each poem's title directly references the respective painting, such as "Said Upon İbrahim Balaban's 'Spring Painting,'" "Ibrahim Balaban's 'Prison Gate Painting'" and "It is said on Balaban's 'Threshing Painting.'" This deliberate inclusion of the painting's title in the poem underscores Hikmet's desire to evoke the essence of Balaban's artworks through language. Moreover, Hikmet extended this tradition of ekphrasis to other artists, notably Abidin Dino, whose painting Walking inspired another poem titled "Said Upon Abidin Dino's Painting Called 'Walking.'" The fact that the title of the poem again mentions the name of the work that is the center of the poem is an indication of the inter-semiotic link he established between painting and poetry. As Nazım Hikmet wrote many poems dedicated to painters or paintings denoting ekphrastic techniques, in his work "Ekphrasis in Nazım Hikmet Poetry" Turgay Anar points out that the poet's body of works includes ten ekphrastic poems directly deriving from visual artworks. He continues: "Nazım Hikmet is the first poet in the history of Turkish literature to write an ekphrastic poem on the cover of a book" (158) referring to *The Cover Picture of a Poetry Book* and he also broke new ground by being the first "to publish a completely ekphrastic poetry book with his *Jokond and Si-Ya-U*" (158) which finds place in Gündüz Vassaf's novel in the third part of the book.

Following the same tradition, İlhan Berk (1918–2008), though primarily recognized as a writer, translator, and poet, also had a profound interest in painting. Despite not identifying himself as a painter, Berk integrated his visual and literary pursuits by painting on the pages of his notebooks and books. In his book *Ekphrasis: Turkey and the West*, Nazmi Ağıl discusses ekphrastic rivalry in Turkish poetry giving several examples including the poem "Şeker Ahmet Pasha: Training Soldiers" by İlhan Berk which, according to his contention "strives to become painting itself" (75). In exemplifying Berk's ability to translate visual art into poetic expression, his poem "Waking up in Paul Klee" which vividly describes Paul Klee's painting *Ad Marginem* can be given another example. Berk's poetry belongs to the Second New Movement, a literary trend characterized by the deferral of explicit meaning, the incorporation of unorthodox imagery, and a call for linguistic innovation.

Bedri Rahmi Eyüboğlu, a versatile artist who lived between 1911 and 1975, was also a writer, poet and painter. Before pursuing his studies in Paris, Bedri Rahmi began painting education at the Academy of Fine Arts. Eyüboğlu's paintings and poems predominantly reflect Anatolian culture featuring elements like manuscripts, rugs, trees and plants native to Anatolia, alongside the region's folk tales. In his art, Eyüboğlu often bridges the themes of painting and poetry. He sometimes creates artworks that are poetic in nature, blending the two genres to form "poetic painting." His unique approach is also visible in his illustrations, where he visually enhances his own poetry books and those of other prominent Turkish poets, such as Orhan Veli and Melih Cevdet Anday. Through his versatile talents, Eyüboğlu has left a lasting impact on both Turkish visual arts and literature, celebrating and preserving Anatolian heritage in multifaceted forms.

The symbiotic relatedness between visual arts and poetry has fostered such a vibrant confluence that it actually transcends cultural and geographical boundaries. Brueghel's paintings, for instance, have influenced foreign poets as well as Turkish poets such as Melih Cevdet Anday and Ülkü Tamer. In his poem "Bruegel," Ülkü Tamer exhibits an ekphrastic expression towards the painter's painting *Hunters in the Snow*. Metin Eloğlu (1927–1985), is another artist who, although known for his literary identity, was also a painter. He also painted portraits of fellow poets such as Edip Cansever and Orhan Veli. Metin Eloğlu included his own drawings in most of his poetry books; one notable example being the book titled *The Boy Afraid of the Rooster* that consists of figurative and abstract black ink drawings. Similarly, Gürkan Coşkun, known as Komet is both a painter and a poet as he has more than two thousand paintings and four published poetry books.

Finally, it is also possible to give examples from some exceptional exhibitions in showcasing the unity and connection between poetry and painting. The exhibition called "Düğün" (Wedding) which was opened at Tem Art Gallery in 2014 encompasses the themes of poetry, painting and architecture highlighting the mutual inspiration and cross-disciplinary influence between poets and artists. Such a thematic exhibition where paintings inspired by the poems are displayed alongside the relevant verses creates a cohesive narrative between literary and visual art mediums. The exhibition brought together a rich and diverse collection of artists and poets; from Edip Cansever, İlhan Berk, Nazım Hikmet, Özdemir Asaf, Ahmet Hamdi Tanpınar, Bedri Rahmi Eyüboğlu, Turgut Uyar to Rainer Maria Rilke, Walt Whitman, Edgar Allen Poe, Rene Char, Arthur Rimbaud and Yannis Ritsos. The artists who brought their unique visual expressions were Komet, Mehmet Güler, Gülden Artun, Nur Özalp, Özlem Özkan, Ekrem Kahraman, Devabil Kara, Zeki Fındıkoğlu, Hüseyin Ertunç, Talat Enlil, Fuat Acaroğlu, Hale Sontaş, Talat Enlil, Nevin İşlek, Ömer Kaleşi and Abdülkadir Özkök. Furthermore, Yüksel Arslan's *Autoartures*[5] *XXIII and XXIV* are included in order to depict Dylan Thomas' "Especially When the October Wind" and "And Death Shall Have No Dominion." The exhibition also has a book published in the same year, prepared by gallery owner Besi Cecan, featuring a preface written by Özdemir İnce. İnce mentions that the words are the tool for the poet, colors and patterns for the painter and notes for the musician (6). Since it is not possible to give the alchemy that transforms a poem into a painting in the mind of the painter, the meaning is not written in the poem, it is in the reader's head, in his imagination (7), hence it is unique. As the composition, in either form, is individual and mysterious, the exhibition evidences how art is dynamic, endless; converges new layers and resonances begetting dialogic, plural platforms.

---

5   "Instead of giving different titles to his works, Yüksel Arslan combined the word "art" with the "ure" suffix in French (like in "peinture" or "écriture") to create the word "arture" and painted his "artures" by plants, herbs, stone, soil, and at times even blood and urine." (https://galerinev.art/en/yuksel-arslan)

Orhan Pamuk's *My Name is Red* and
The Naive and Sentimental Novelist

Novel as a literary genre does not have a long history in Turkey. During the Tanzimat Period, as the cultural relations with Europe gained momentum, some foreign-language intellectuals translated the works into Turkish making them accessible to everyone. Some writers, deriving from these translations and European literary tendencies, attempted to pen their works in a similar manner. As novel as genre was very popular in Europe, it garnered significant attention in Turkey as well. 2006 Nobel Literature Prize winner Orhan Pamuk's 1998 novel *My Name is Red (Benim Adım Kırmızı)* is not only a remarkable novel in intertwining visual art and storytelling, but it also delves into the world of miniature art, sixteenth century Ottoman Empire which is relevant to the history of visual narratives in Turkish literature. Thus, the novel is congruous in understanding the historical and artistic context which is important in setting the foundation for exploring contemporary novels that epitomize art and text complementation. On the other hand, his treatise or reflections on art and writing from Charles Eliot Norton Lectures at Harvard University are compiled in the book *The Naive and Sentimental Novelist (Saf ve Düşünceli Romancı)* which provides a valuable insight into how visual imagery meets narrative imagination. What Pamuk reflects at length is "associating a novelist with a painter and the novel with a landscape painting" (Uysal 437). Therefore, *My name is Red* is a clear and pertinent manifestation of that formulation.

My Name is Red revolves around murder mystery of artists who are commissioned by the sultan to create an illustrated book yet with the employment of new artistic and technical styles reminiscent of Italian Renaissance. The fear, anxiety and ultimate murders among the artists serve as a testament to a broader context of cultural tension between the East and West as the established norms and representations of Islamic traditions are at stake. In that sense the novel has great relevance to cultural and artistic conflicts encountered throughout history particularly resonating with Gülsoy's novel which also explores transitions in art from traditional to modern forms.

In *The Naive and Sentimental Novelist,* Orhan Pamuk says that painting and literature are intertwined, "writing a novel means painting with words, and reading a novel means visualizing images through someone else's words" (93). Likewise, in the novel *My Name is Red*, Enishte defines the miniature as a book painting, actually a painting without a story is unthinkable for him. While talking to Black, he says, "Every painting tells a story. To beautify the book we read, the painter paints the most beautiful assembly of the story." (33). Pamuk is one of those few writers painting with words, harnessing from words and pictures equally. As the art of writing a novel entails an "ability to perceive the thoughts and sensations of protagonists within a landscape" (89) he admits how the first step for him is formation of a picture, an image in his mind (93).

In his historical novel, Orhan Pamuk explores the clash between East and West within artistic traditions delving into approaches to art with a special focus on the problem of perspective in a philosophical and cultural context. Although in some cultures, perspective is not prioritized because it creates an illusion, in Islam, depiction in perspective is a taboo, for fear of a return to iconoclasm. Islam forbids realist painting because it sees it as a blasphemous attempt to create; given that creation is reserved for God alone. Such an approach naturally stifles the art of painting in Muslim societies. Therefore, Pamuk examines the consequences of the prohibition on the art of painting as well as its effects on the psychological formation of people raised in Muslim societies.

My Name is Red is set in Istanbul, the capital of the sixteenth century Ottoman Empire, with anachronistically organized events and characters. Pamuk transcends traditional storytelling by allowing not only characters but also objects and concepts to narrate their experiences in the first person which enables an unconventional perspective shaped by its own space and time. Apart from the objects, the figures depicted in the miniatures of the main characters are also given voice as they speak about the art of miniature painting. At this point, the novel presents a highly innovative narrative structure and provides information and commentary on the visual and intellectual fiction of the miniature. As miniature denotes a form of visual narrative complementing the text, Pamuk develops his novel within the framework of analyzing the statements and descriptions of Ottoman miniatures, which constitute the backbone of the story. The sections in the novel about miniatures and the painters give insight into the dominant understanding of depiction in the Islamic world illuminating the historical context and the nature of artistic creation. An immediate connection to the art of miniature is also found in the construction of the novel which is based on using multiple perspectives. In Islamic tradition, miniature has a unique form in visualizing the text, thereby creating a multifaceted viewpoint. The fact that Western painting generally leans on central perspective builds a sharp contrast and accordingly in *My Name is Red*, having different characters as a narrative technique, mirrors miniatures depicting multiple scenes within a single composition. Such a narrative approach highlights the novel's exploration of miniature painting, both thematically and formally, making its treatment of miniatures particularly notable.

During the Ottoman Empire, the production of miniature manuscripts, which reached its peak during the reign of Murad III (1574–1595), especially from the second half of the sixteenth century onwards, gained a documentary quality with the depiction of daily life and ceremonies. This period, during which palace life was depicted and illustrated in manuscripts, corresponds to the time period in which *My Name is Red* takes place. According to Kırca's contention: "This specific period of the Ottoman history when miniature art reached its maturity while Venetian pictorial art produced the best examples of linear perspective drawing in Europe is fictionalized and comes to constitute the novel's focal point." (37). As discussed in the previous section on Ottoman miniature art, the transition encountered in Mehmed II's reign during which he commissioned his portrait marks a departure from traditional Islamic conventions and recognition of western techniques like perspective. The major conflict in the novel, which leads to the murder, also arises from a desire to transform classical miniature art. Therefore, the shifts in art and literature parallel broader changes in political, economic and religious domains of the time reflecting the prevailing understanding and mentality. Furthermore, Kırca believes that "Pamuk's *My Name is Red* evolves into the image text in which the visual representation is verbally narrated" (39). Therefore, while what is visual is transformed into textual, what is written is also transformed into pictorial dissolving the paragonal relationship between word and image or poetry and painting.

Miniature by itself is beyond a simple illustration or symbolic representation and in a similar manner, in establishing a relation between painting and narrative, Pamuk's novel "contains a two-dimensional dialogue: the first is the East-West dialogue that is attempted to be created by presenting forgotten Eastern art with a Western discourse, and the second is the past-present dialogue that exists in postmodernism" (Uzundemir 118). Metafictional approach of the novel not only offers readers a new way to revisit the forgotten values of the past and make a historical evaluation of *the nakkash* but also blends Eastern and Western traditions, methods, habits and histories which is the hallmark Pamuk owes the wealth of his narratives. The author engages with the principles of miniature to such an extent that, it is projected onto the multi-layered and multi-perspective structure of the novel. With an ekphrastic re-imagination, word and image are intertwined creating a hybridity in the form of a confluence where western word and eastern image meet. Establishing a different connection between miniature/painting and narrative, *My Name is*

Red presents the art of the East/Islam with a Western discourse and constructs its story with intertextual abstractions by establishing the East-West dialog within this perspective. Therefore, before exploring the novels in detail, it is important to recognize the significance of Pamuk's two specific works as pioneering studies in creative writing and visual narrative.

Chapter 2
Painter Vasif's History of Secret Loves
by Murat Gülsoy

Creative Writing

Murat Gülsoy seems to be engaging deeply with the nature of fiction in his works giving hints how he constructs stories revealing the process of writing. Such a shift towards metafiction marks broader philosophical and aesthetic understanding as the focus is on how reality is constructed rather than representing reality. Thus, "pure artistic creativity" in both form and content becomes the main goal in the author's mind. In short, instead of fictionalizing concrete life, the literary text begins to narrate its own fiction. The stimulating factors to write an artist novel for Murat Gülsoy is not only the interest in the years when modern painting was born and developed in Turkey which also becomes the founding years of the country, but also reflecting on the art of painting is pivotal considering that elaborations on painting equals to thinking on the representation of reality. Drawing his major inspiration from the question "how does a mind work?" Gülsoy delves into the writing process and the importance of literature in the creativity of the human mind. In order to write, fictionalize or create, one has to utilize the mind in the highest regard and accordingly Gülsoy has been organizing seminars on creative writing at various institutions, especially Boğaziçi University.

In his work *Ekphrasis: Turkey and the West*, Nazmi Ağıl remarks how "Gülsoy makes use of the power of pictures to inspire writing" (190) reminding of the fact that Gülsoy has been conducting workshops using ekphrasis in creative writing courses. When asked about the unbreakable bond between literature and other branches of art, Gülsoy says: "all arts are in contact with each other, but in particular painting and literature are very close".[6] In another interview he even admits that painting proceeds novels and stories.[7] His fascination and engagement with paintings are best manifested in one of his earlier novels, *A Week of Kindness in Istanbul (İstanbul'da Bir Merhamet Haftası)*, published in 2007. Gülsoy fictionalizes the novel around seven surreal paintings of collages by Max Ernst. The starting point for him is looking at those strange pictures and realizing that they could not be translated into textual language. Thus, he comes up with the idea of showing these pictures to seven different characters and recording their experiences through their own lens and language. Murat Gülsoy's another novel *Can God See Me? (Tanrı Beni Görüyor mu?)* features four different photographs and

---

6   https://www.literaedebiyat.com/post/ressam-vasif-in-gizli-asklar-tarihi-murat-gulsoy-soylesi

7   https://sanatkritik.com/soylesi/murat-gulsoy-elbette-gayriresmi-oldukca-oznel-bir-tarih-anlatisi-bu/

four different stories written under them. As Köker indicates in her article, one of the major factors that transforms these photographs into fiction is that they have an imaginative appearance as every image has its own, unique way of being seen that emerges when impressions and experiences from the outside world are reinterpreted and reproduced in the mind (1946). Apart from his novels, Gülsoy also penned *Disenchantment: Creative Writing (Büyübozumu: Yaratıcı Yazarlık)* in 2004 which is a testament to the issues he addresses in his creative writing workshops. In the book, Gülsoy chronicles the elements of fiction, what creative writing is, whether it can be taught, how the stories are generated and narrated, the use and importance of time, place, plot, character and point of view. Giving examples from his own journey as a writer, Gülsoy talks about the ritual of writing highlighting the fact that his aim is not mapping out methods but rather pointing the challenges that writers encounter stylistically from the title to the organization of the book. Although fiction has no formulas to be memorized or applied, Gülsoy addresses that the best way to flesh out characters is not summarizing who there are but showing them in action (5). In that sense "dialogues allow the readers to see and hear the characters directly" (6). As the commentary of the narrator is an already abandoned technique in modern literature, what is expected from the readers is an active interaction and participation through their own interpretations to the created-fictionalized world of the writer. In a similar sense, in her highly detailed biographical search on the writer, Mahinur Akşehir defines Gülsoy's approach to art as "an act of soul-searching" (128) which puts sincerity in such a high esteem that it also motivates the readers to become participants in that quest.

While comparing story with novel and painting with sculpture. Gülsoy draws an anology between painting and novel as in both cases, it is hard to "see" at first glance. For that reason, by blending visual art with storytelling, it is possible to create unique narratives for readers as exemplified in both novels. Imagining a story and wondering the intriguing question whether that story can create its own reality amounts to staying in a limbo, somewhere between fiction and reality. Gülsoy creates a similar situation in his narrative as the boundaries blur suggesting that the act of storytelling has the power to shape and redefine what is perceived as real. The writer is particularly interested in harmonizing personal experiences with creative endeavors and the ways in which personal histories intersect with broader historical narratives.

Even the name Gülsoy chooses for his character, Vasıf Ekrem Yelda sounds very convincing and authentic; feels historically and culturally appropriate. As the journalist is recording Vasıf's life story, Vasıf is simultaneously making a portrait of the journalist. As he transfers him into the canvas, he actually delves into the intricacies of his features and expression, imagining a life for him which equals to what Gülsoy is doing in writing the novel. Likewise, art, especially portraiture provides a unique way to explore complexities of human experience and identity as the dynamic nature of artistic process allows adding further layers and personal insights moving beyond astute, physical depictions. A portrait is actually the deepest way to get to know a person and it is as much about the artist as it is about the subject.

Gülsoy also brings a different dimension to *künstlerroman,* German term generally associated with artist novels in which the story is shaped around the evolution of an artist in a fictional world. Distinctively he creates a fictional character in a real world. As a matter of fact, it is observed that the artistic adventure of the artist in the *künstlerroman* does not always follow a classical line of growth-development-maturation; in such novels the artist goes through a complicated and compelling phase in the process of becoming an artist and practicing his art both in an individual and social sense. The painter Vasıf is a hero wandering among the real stories of the real names of our painting history. The novel, which evolves from Paris to Istanbul and many European cities, offers a special narrative of both the historical transformation of Turkey and the adventure of modern Turkish painting. Driven by a desire to depict a specific period through a painter character, Gülsoy masterfully blends fiction with reality: the fictitious character Vasıf is crafted through a self-reflexive fusion of concrete reality and imaginative transformation. It even becomes challenging at some points to distinguish between the real and the imaginary or the historical and the fictional. Gülsoy bases his novel as a tribute to those who founded and developed modern art of painting in Turkey which explains the inclusion of so many real, historical figures in the novel intertwining the reality and fiction at some points. The novel is woven not only with real people and events, but also presents a wealth of documents and materials in the gallery sections. Hence Gülsoy uses the term documentary novel in order to indicate the hybrid structure of the novel.

Moreover, that inter-genre of the novel gains another dimension with the help of artificial intelligence programs as Gülsoy uses Midjourney in order to create the picture on the cover and the rotating pictures in the novel's promotional video thereby offering another hybridity through the blend of imagination and technological novelties. In an increasingly digitalized world, the relationship between the literariness and the digital is so multifaceted that it offers innovative narrative activities giving rise to new forms in storytelling prompting more engagement from the readers. In his own words Gülsoy narrates the process in the interview made by Doğuş Sarpkaya:

> I had to determine a drawing style according to Vasıf's life cycle. For example, he will go to Paris and be influenced by the art scene there. Then he will come back to occupied Istanbul, draw orientalist paintings and sell them to foreign commanders and embassy officials. He will draw aging Fatma Belkıs in his notebook with charcoal, walk around Istanbul and keep a record of the streets. I had all these in my mind and they are already in the novel. I entered all these data and had the artificial intelligence draw them.[8]

Using AI tools to create images based on provided textual input has already found application in many creative domains like music, architecture, fine arts and visual storytelling. Such generative models impact the creative process and provide the artists or writers like Gülsoy, with new ideas, styles and technologies. As AI programs make their way into creative process more and more, traditional artistic practices gain new horizons as co-created artworks assist pushing boundaries stressing the interplay between artistic expression and technological novelties.

Painter Vasıf's retrospective booklet, which brings together examples of his paintings and drawings throughout his life, was also a product of the same artificial intelligence. For the novel on painter Vasıf, he narrates how an exhibition on Giacometti deeply inspired him to design a novel like an exhibition catalog. In the gallery section at the end of each chapter, Gülsoy presents visual transcriptions describing the documents in Vasıf's archive. The fact that these images are not photographs not only challenges the reader's imagination, but also opens the doors to a world of fiction where it is not clear whether they are in color or black and white. It is possible to follow the development of Turkish painting throughout the novel, so it could be inferred that the novel turns into a history of painting as a sourcebook. In this way, the book focuses on the portraits of important figures who experimented in different fields of art history, art sociology and aesthetics, bringing to the fore many visual artists, gallerists and art critics. The common characteristic of these creators is that their works and endeavors did not receive the attention they deserved during their lifetimes and afterwards. Gülsoy's fictionalization technique in dealing with these figures is based, above all, on complete and accurate historical information. This meticulous approach reveals that the author has shaped the figures through a deep documentary research, gathered a great deal of information and constructed their relationship with Vasıf based on historical facts.

---

8   https://www.literaedebiyat.com/post/ressam-vasif-in-gizli-asklar-tarihi-murat-gulsoy-
    soylesi

Who Is Painter Vasıf?

In the fall of 1967, Vasıf Ekrem Yelda, a forgotten painter, begins to tell Ali Halit Doğan, a young journalist, about his life. Beginning in an attic in Moda, Vasıf's voice recordings unveil the darkest details of a modern painter who lived between 1889 and 1968. Born in a mansion in Çamlıca, Vasıf's first contact with the art of painting is thanks to his uncle Tevfik Rüstem, a military physician and an amateur painter. He receives his basic painting education from the painter Viçen Arslanyan while studying at Mekteb-i Sultani. Between 1909 and 1914, he works in Paris in the studio of Georgette Valané, whom he calls "my real master." Upon his return to Istanbul, his uncle Ali Salih Pasha, his nephew Fazıl, his wife Fatma Belkıs and their child Orhan Necmi enter his life. At various periods of his life, he teaches at Galatasaray High School and the Academy, crosses paths with painters such as Feyhaman Duran, Nazmi Ziya, İbrahim Çallı, Alexis Gritchenko, Fikret Mualla, Bedri Rahmi Eyüboğlu and Aliye Berger, but keeps away from being associated with any school or group, finally opening his first solo exhibition at Adalet Cimcoz's Maya Art Gallery. While Vasıf Ekrem Yelda's friendships with many important painters from Bedri Rahmi to Nazmi Ziya, from İbrahim Çallı to Feyhaman Duran provide an informal historical narrative of the history of Turkish painting, the relationships Vasıf developed with all these names draw a different picture of the history of modern Turkish painting through his eyes. For the painter Vasıf, the history of painting is the story of a painful artistic struggle full of disappointments, reflecting the efforts of modernization. With this book on the history of painting, Gülsoy not only brings many forgotten painters to light, but also highlights the sacrifices and efforts made by artists to navigate the changing artistic landscapes and societal expectations providing insights into the complexity of artistic pursuits in the country within a historical and cultural context.

Painter Vasıf was born in Istanbul in the late 1880s, in the era of the empire, and died in the late 1960s, in the era of the republic. In his 80 years of life, he witnesses two world wars, the collapse of the empire, the establishment of a new state, the September 6–7 incidents and the Coup of 60. Accordingly, Gülsoy widens the scope of his novel as the evolutions of the painter are also in compliance with the historical and social developments in the country. All the great literary figures that he is somehow associated with are the prominent artists who bestride the art of painting and poetry which is widely encountered in artistic endeavors. In conjunction with that, at the beginning of the novel, Vasıf compares the art of painting with literature and music in order to stress its uniqueness.

> Painting is such an ungrateful art. If it were a novel, there would definitely be an edition of it in a library, it would be reprinted one day, if it were a symphony, even if it was forgotten, someone would find its notes one day and play it again, it wouldn't disappear. But painting is not like that. Even if you photograph it, it is not the same. It is not the same at all. (115–116)

Although the art of painting or the act of painting is unique for Vasıf, the feeling it gives, embodies a multifaceted nature that explains why even his signature has never been fixed; sometimes Vasıf, sometimes Vasıf Ekrem Yelda, or just Yelda. Rather than a path to fame, painting amalgamates several lifelines to clung in order to survive for him.

> The feeling of being one! That is the essence of art. The interesting thing is that is also the essence of being human. To be unique, to be like no other. Isn't it true that every human being is different from one another? This is the law of life… Man imagines himself as something unique. This feeling is strongest in the artist. I felt so unique that afternoon when I was painting Tragic Mustafa Çelebi in the garden of the sluggish lodge in Karacaahmet. I felt so unique. Indeed, at that moment, there was only one Karacaahmet Cemetery in the world, there was only one leper Mustafa Çelebi in that lodge, and there was only one person painting him: Me! The young painter Vasıf. I felt this very strongly. In fact, I always feel this when I paint, without exception: Being unique. This feeling starts the moment I pick up the brush or the pen. It's as if one cannot be unique while eating, drinking tea, washing face, taking the ferry, chatting with friends, or doing any other task. It is a marvelous state that only occurs when I paint. (86–87)

While mentioning how his works were belittled as nothing more than an imitation or illustration, Vasıf hinges upon the criteria of appreciation in our country, how the identification of the new is based upon being acknowledged in foreign countries reinforcing further questions on the misconceptions on the factor of originality. The fact that associations with the innovative in Turkey often relies on validation from foreign countries underscores the complexity of dynamics with Turkish art scene. This dependence on external appreciation is not the only point highlighted by Gülsoy as a challenge but the societal tendency to perceive artists as unconventional or eccentric projects a juncture between uniqueness and madness as the disconnect between artistic expression and societal expectations raises questions on the stereotypes that often lead artists being labeled as mad due to their disposition in challenging norms.

On the issue of madness, Vasıf reminds the invisible factor that because artists are people who push the boundaries, they are often at odds with the general public; their work is considered strange, and they are therefore labeled "mad". Vasıf's observations shed light on the toggles faced by many artists yet on the other hand, there are artists who struggle in the grip of delusions and genuinely suffer from mental illnesses. At this point, Gülsoy comments: "Look… You mentioned Fikret Mualla, he is a different case. His madness was also very different. Maybe the life he lived made him mad. Or the life he couldn't live. He is a great artist, but no one appreciates him" (106). The thin line between artistic brilliance and mental instability has been often explored through the lives of many renowned artists like Van Gogh, Salvador Dali, Edvard Munch who produced iconic works despite suffering from severe mental problems. As referenced in the first part of the book, tracing the roots of art "romanticises artists and shamans as individuals who are somehow, perhaps via such vague terms as 'genius' or 'neurosis', uniquely connected to a special or dangerous realm of inspiration" (Wallis 5) from prehistorical times to today. Accordingly, Gülsoy reminds of a familiar and fitting figure from Turkish history of painting as Fikret Mualla whose turbulent and extraordinary life alternated between madness and genius. While in Paris, for more than three years, Vasıf also lives with a mad painter named Georgette whose breakdowns would last for days. Exclaiming that her soul is rotting in a dark dungeon, Georgette would even tear up her own paintings. Vasıf not only becomes an apprentice for her but he would also go from being a student to a lover or friend. Vasıf questions: "Who was I, what was I, what was I doing there? Was I a student of a modern artist or an apprentice to a mad painter? Was I the lover of an old woman? Was I caught up in an oedipal fantasy?" (111–112). His years in Paris, which are mostly characterized by vacillations on identity and belonging, remind him of young Turkish artists who also came to this city to learn the art of painting. "Art is the child of mythological story and personal experience. At least that's what I have learned from Georgette" (113). For Vasıf, the way two individuals come together in a unique way in love has analogy to appreciating and interpreting art in terms of bringing personal and subjective perspectives and experiences. The encounter with an art work also resonates with a similar connection in shaping the emotions and perceptions as the two inner worlds or subjectivities are coincided. Vasıf remembers his first time in Paris, at Louvre and how he felt years later, as after painting hundreds of paintings himself he could understand what he was capable of when he looks at them with a different eye. He expounds that he could now sense the artists' state of mind; their worries, their sadness, their ambitions, sometimes their joy, even imagining the place where they painted, their studios or their streets.

In his book *Disenchantment: Creative Writing*, Gülsoy comments that "the characters we create exist for their own stories" (15) in that the narrating character does not act like a puppet solely designed/created to invoice the writer. He rather thinks that the best way is providing the character with a past. "Whether it is a story or novel, if you want your characters resemble real people, you must first create a "life story" for them" (17). Accordingly, Gülsoy does not just surround his character with real historical personages in order to project the art scene in the country with utmost precision but he also creates a storyline concerning his familial relationships. At this point retrospective booklet created through an AI program provides a valuable insight into Vasif's personal experiences, emotions and hidden aspects of his life. In designing a past or background for the character, envisioning the family he was born into is equally significant in perceiving his socio-economic status in uncovering layers of meaning and enriching the overall thematic exploration of his identity. The texts used in the catalog, compiled from the paintings and sketches he made during various periods of his life of ups and downs, are excerpted from the novel. At the beginning of the catalog, as expected from an artist who witnessed different periods such as the Constitutional Monarchy, the World Wars and the Republic, there are mostly landscape paintings with the themes of Istanbul, the Bosphorus, fishermen and birds in accordance with the first examples of Turkish painting. One of those series is called Istanbul neighborhoods which of course includes Tarabya, Küçüksu, Moda, Çamlıca, Rumelihisarı, Süleymaniye, Karaköy, Salacak, Tophane, Karacaahmet and Taksim Square. "My intention was both to paint the old Istanbul, to capture its last lights before they disappeared, and to tell the story of the new Istanbul. Women and men in modern clothes in patisseries, in squares, at the harbor, on the train platform…" (166). Thus, the catalog not only unveils the artist's evolving perspectives but such a visual and artistic journey also mirrors broader shifts and transformations in Turkish culture.

Vasif's relatives, his uncle Ali Salih Pasha, his nephew Fazıl, his wife Fatma Belkıs and their children Orhan Necmi, are the figures who accompany the narrative in different periods from the beginning to the end of the novel. The night his uncle Ali Salih Pasha dies is pivotal as when he is summoned to the mansion, he immediately visualizes the whole scene in pictorial and painterly details.

> The view I saw looked more like a Vermeer painting. In the dim light the room looked bigger than it really was. A heaviness expanding infinitely from dark corners, death. Ali Salih Pasha's body, which had not yet solidified, was free of aches and pains, and in a peaceful silence, he was in the last stages of his existence. (159–160)

The darkness of the night serves as a metaphor for the shadows cast by past secrets and unresolved emotions within the family as Vasif learns that Orhan Necmi is actually born out of an affair between Fatma Belkıs and his uncle Ali Salih years ago. For Vasif, the tragic events surrounding the revelation of Orhan Necmi's true parentage is not limited with losing Fatma Belkıs but devastated Orhan Necmi burns down the house in Çamlıca causing many of the paintings to be gone as well. The basic principles of Vasıf's art are most lucidly revealed through his family affairs or secrets as the black-and-white sketches in which he depicts Fatma Belkıs in front of the window with her back turned in reference to the years they did not see each other, are also striking in the catalog. For Vasıf, Fatma Belkıs is probably the most important woman in his life, not only as a secret love, unspoken passion, muse or mother figure but also supplies him with an emotional intensity that is emblematic of his more comprehensive approach to art and life in general. In fact, Fatma Belkıs evokes and recaptures Vasıf's mentor Georgette who, as previously mentioned, has a similar function tendering a complex net of relationships.

Vasıf's personal relationships revolving around love and desire anchor his artistic journey as he does not make a particular choice in his adventures between both male and female partners. For example, the works in the catalog depicting male models with flower crowns on their heads, reminiscent of Bacchus from Roman mythology, are also noteworthy. It is easily inferred that the half-naked male model in these paintings is Jean whom Georgette also uses as model for her works delving into themes of mythology and sensuality. The androgynous Bacchus, the Roman god of wine, ecstasy and madness is equivalent to Greek god Dionysus and has appeared in various depictions of famous painters like Caravaggio and Rubens. Vasıf remembers how Georgette used Jean's body to show the intricacies of human anatomy. He recalls how he would falter while touching intimate parts of Jean's Greek-statue like body and Georgette would encourage him which would ultimately lead Jean to fall into ecstasy as his whimpers would be invitatory to the gardens of sweetest sins (114). He hints that those scenes would possibly end in erotic, sexual intercourses with the influence of wine. The associations of eroticism and homosexuality within a mythological and artistic context transpire in Vasıf's personal experiences finding visual resonances in the section entitled "art has no limits" which is poignant in intersecting art and pleasure. Strikingly, the ending words on the back cover of the exhibition catalog are "creation, death and pleasure." Considering that Vasıf has a series entitled "Apocalypse" which are inspired by some scary folk and fairy tale figures that he filters through his childhood memories and even puts one specific painting, *An Ordinary Day after the Apocalypse*, in the gallery section provokes the writer's reflections on those concepts and the intricate liaisons between them. The painting depicts an old angel crying under an olive tree. A woman, wearing a tuxedo jacket, with her umbilical cord dangling from her crotch is informing the old angel that the apocalypse has come (307). With such an imagery laden with symbolism, Gülsoy might be beckoning the juxtaposition between apocalypse which is the death and destruction and umbilical cord, typically associated with birth and beginning. Ironically Vasıf rates the series as his best and relates how he enjoyed making them.

Group D Painters in Turkey

Gülsoy creates such a character that he is aware of the importance of the dynamic junctures found in art as form of inspiration. Although Gülsoy opts not to locate his character in a certain artistic group, the associations with some figures inevitably connote lucid affiliations not only from Vasıf's life story but also from Turkish modernization acts in art. With the modernization movement initiated by the Ottoman Empire in its last century, talented young artists were sent to Europe to receive education who ultimately returned to the country seeking ways to create art as unique as possible. Within this search, the most effective effort at originality was made by the artists who defined themselves as Group D and opened many exhibitions across the country to socialize art and create cultural change. In order to create our own original art, they synthesized local traditional motifs and patterns with the formal understanding of contemporary painting.

Before discussing Group D, which constitutes one of the most important turning points of modern Turkish painting, it is necessary to discuss the Generation of Military Painters, Sanayi Nefise School (Academy of Fine Arts), the Ottoman Painters' Society, the painters of the 1914 Generation and the Independent Union of Painters and Sculptors in a chronological sense as Vasıf emphasizes how their influence is beyond identical copies coming out of one another as each artist takes something from the other, shapes it and adds his own personality to it. It is important to note that military school had significant share in initiating formal art education in a Western sense. As referenced in the first part, during the nineteenth century, traditional experiments in painting and concerted efforts in Military schools gave impetus to the transition to a Western understanding of painting. These military institutions, which began incorporating painting courses into their curricula as early as 1793 at the Mühendishâne-i Berri-i Hümâyun (Imperial School of Military Engineering), had a profound impact on civilian schools.

> Mühendishane-ı Berri Hümayun, one of the first institutions established in the Ottoman Empire to provide education in the western sense, was founded in 1795. Among the students at the school, where military engineering education was given, students with a tendency towards the art of painting emerged. These students formed the generation of painters who would later be recognized as painters of military. (Baysal 31)

The developments in military education, particularly the inclusion of painting classes, influenced civilian institutions, and the introduction of foreign painting instructors further accelerated these advancements. Therefore, the painting lessons initiated at the Mühendishâne-i Berri-i Hümâyun are considered the inception of painting education in Turkey. Among the most notable representatives were İbrahim Paşa, Şeker Ahmet Ali Paşa and Osman Hamdi who ushered in the foundation of Sanayi-i Nefise School, a fine arts school in 1883. The first group of painters established in the Ottoman Empire under the presidency of Sami Yetik to address the problems of art and artists is the "Ottoman Society of Painters." Young painters such as Hikmet Onat, İbrahim Çallı, Agâh Bey, Mehmet Ruhi Arel, Ahmet Ziya Akbulut, Halil Paşa, Hüseyin Zekai Paşa, Nazmi Ziya Güran, Hüseyin Avni Lifij, Feyhaman Duran, Mehmet Ali Laga and Müfide Kadri were influential in the establishment of the society. Sent to Paris in 1910, these young artists had to return to Istanbul in 1914 at the outbreak of World War I and became known as the painters of the 1914 Generation with their unique style. The 1914 Generation, which succeeded in reflecting the excitement of the impressionist understanding of painting in their art, was followed by another important organization of painters, the Independent Union of Painters and Sculptors, founded by painters who were sent abroad in 1924 and returned in 1928.

The historical development of modern Turkish painting entered a new phase with the establishment of Group D in 1933 which was formed by Nurullah Berk, Zeki Faik İzer, Elif Naci, Cemal Tollu, Abidin Dino and Zühtü Müridoğlu. As the painters were the fourth group established until that date, they chose the name "D," the fourth letter of the Latin alphabet. When the works of Group D artists, most of whom grew up as students of İbrahim Çallı and his friends at the Sanayi-i Nefise School, are examined, their unique stylistic differences immediately stand out. Influenced by art movements like Fauvism, Cubism and Expressionism, these artists tried to create new syntheses from the combination of the local and the universal as they aspired to express the east-west synthesis pictorially. For that reason, since the 1940s, they produced works in accordance with the local folkloric artistic motifs and stylized them in their own artistic style which caused an interaction diversifying their artistic creativity. Besides as Genç remarks, "when Turgut Zaim and Bedri Rahmi Eyüboğlu joined Group D in 1934, the artists began to show interest in local motifs and themes." (413). Thus, the members of the group tried to give Turkish painting an identity through interpretations that synthesized tradition and modernity, taking technique from the West and content from the cultural climate.

Vasıf is also very interested in Group D, the first painting ecole of the republic. Upon hearing the death news of some of those painters who were not deservedly appreciated, Vasıf elaborates that painting is the most unfortunate art in Turkey with a history of just hundred years. At the funeral of Ali Sami, he thinks how Fikret Mualla died in foreign lands, Nazmi Ziya who was totally dedicated to his art but could not see the fruits of his great labor or İbrahim Çallı who enigmatically never had an individual exhibition in spite of being a popular painter in the country. At this point, he narrates an interesting anecdote concerning Çallı and Atatürk, the founder of Turkish Republic, which could provide glimpses into Atatürk's personality and appreciation for art. Vasıf underlies the fact that Çallı is the only artist among Group D to have painted a portrait of Atatürk. He remarks:

> When he went to paint him, he asked him, "Tell me, Çallı, are you going to paint my image or the Atatürk you have?" When Çallı said, "The Atatürk I have," he said, "Well, then you don't need me," and he skipped the pose. He turned to his aide and told him not to bargain, but to pay half of whatever he said. (172)

Vasıf further underscores the leader's keen awareness for authenticity and realism in another instance which features Çallı's famous painting *Zeibeks*. For Vasıf, Atatürk's initial reaction to the painting not only proves his smartness but also highlights his focus on art to reflect realities faithfully. On the beauty of the painting, Vasıf narrates how "it actually reflects the spirit of that period well. The day slowly brightening over the dark mountain ranges in the background, anxious but determined zeibeks, peasant women with serious expressions… They are making preparations. They are loading a horse" (172–173). But the captivating moment is when Atatürk asks: "We couldn't find bread to eat back then, how did this horse get so fat?" (173). In response to such an acute observation, Çallı immediately emaciates the horses with a few brush strokes. Çallı may have wanted to emphasize a particular narrative of historical context but given the challenges and sufferings faced during that period, Atatürk's intervention reflects a commitment to ensure that future generations remember the sacrifices made for the country.

Art, Politics and Women

One notable aspect of the evolution of the Turkish painting concerns the lack of political identity or how limited the role of the politics is in the artists' works. In Aytül Papila's view during the Westernization, the artists from upper class were already indifferent to addressing social or economic problems while those from middle or lower classes did not have the courage to criticize society (132). The shift in the approach to art especially when the Democratic Party came to power illustrates the clashes in ideologies and perception. Vasıf refers to an exhibition opened in Ankara in 1956 and how the minister of education, Tevfik İleri fiercely and negatively reacts to the depictions of poverty, misery in the paintings. In another incident, the president of the parliament Koraltan's anger over the presence of a donkey picture in the parliament, which was made by Orhan Peker, underscores the tensions between artistic autonomy and political dynamics in Turkey at the time (276).

At that point, Vasıf makes an allusion to Virginia Woolf's idea of a room of one's own which is very relevant to artistic pursuits of both men and women equally in our country. "In order to engage in art, one must have minimum conditions. As Virginia Woolf said… Right… She said it for women, a writer should have a room of her own. But in our country, this is true for all artists, men and women alike. Of course, when it's a woman, you have to multiply it by two or three" (291). Throughout history, the disparity between recognition and opportunity for women compared to men is mostly highlighted in the challenges and constraints faced by many women who had little or no access to professional education in art. Exceptional talents like Artemisia Gentileschi, who managed to rise above limits is largely due to her father who was also a painter as the common pathway for women at the time to pursue art was only through being born into a family of artists or marrying into one as evidenced in the following comments by Şentürk:

> Similar to the fact that Mary Shelley, the author of *Frankenstein, or the Modern Prometheus* (1818), grew up in a family and environment that provided her with resources, intellectualism, and the opportunity to follow new writings and developments in literature and philosophy, Artemisia's ability to paint is due to the fact that her father Orazio Gentileschi was a painter and the period she lived in embraced art and artists. (146)

As a reflection of that Vasıf refers to two women painters in Turkey; Mihri Müşfik and Hale Asaf. After the second half of the nineteenth century, the idea of increasing women's participation in social life through education, introduced by the Tanzimat, had a great influence on the emergence of the female figure in Turkish painting. This new female identity was embodied in the life and works of Mihri Müşfik (1886–1954), the first Turkish woman painter. The opportunities and freedom provided by her father, Mehmet Rasim Pasha, were decisive in the artist's life as she took private lessons in Istanbul in order to become a painter, and continued her art education in Rome and Paris. Once again, a familial advantage plays a crucial role in procuring the freedom necessary for artistic aspirations which was very uncommon for the women of her era. In that sense, Müşfik not only broke barriers in a male dominated profession, she also had a pioneering role in advocating for the rights of women in art scene, encouraging her students to explore new techniques like painting outdoors or working with both female and male models.

Towards the end of the book, Gülsoy proposes a similar item for the agenda of women, art and politics. The painting competition organized by Yapı Kredi Bank in 1954 determines "Production" as the topic. Aliye Berger's ultimate triumph signifies a rupture against the established academic norms as Gülsoy, in particular focuses on the traditional evaluation criteria in the country and how it was defied and deconstructed. Berger's composition features a huge sun surrounded by people, "but they seem to be invisible in the strong light of the sun, and in one corner there are villagers, fishermen and so on" (Gülsoy 295). Vasıf's perspective, narrating the events suggests the complexities of art criticism and cultural perceptions as what is harshly criticized is not only the outcome of the competition but also the fact that the jury members were foreign art critics. Yet what cannot go unnoticed is that the foreign jury has no preconceptions, and they are equally unfamiliar with the paintings. Vasıf sees no harm in acknowledging that Berger would not have won if the jury consisted of local members. Vasıf is angered at seeing that even close friends like Bedri Rahmi are extremely critical of the result. For him the history of Turkish painting already spans only fifty years of evolution when compared to international standards. Vasıf sees the controversy surrounding the competition and the disappointment of many artists as an awakening to confront the realities given that they are unable to meet the expectations of foreign experts which contradicts their assumptions that they are part of the world of Western masters.

On the other hand, a woman winning the competition underlies the gender biases: "On top of that, a woman you do not take seriously made the greatest painting, and you can't accept that! Academia is important, so is education, but if you limit art with only one school and the world of a few teachers, this is how you hit the wall!" (297). Vasıf even finds a mythical and symbolic example with a reference to judges from Olympus saying "you are accepted by the society but suddenly three judges from Olympus, from whom you stole the fire, come and test you and you fail" (303). The complexity of artistic validation not only centers on overcoming cultural barriers or struggling against numerous odds in establishing one's identity but the gap between the transformation of the image of woman and the lack of female artists is equally significant. In her work "Where did women go? Female Artists from the Ottoman Empire to the Early Years of the Turkish Republic," Shaw draws attention to "the eagerness to educate women artists and the perils of their participation in the professional art" (22) giving many examples including Mihri Müşfik, Hale Asaf and Aliye Berger. Although the increase in the visibility of women artists in the artistic field designate a positive aspect of modernization, fostering an inclusive environment where women can thrive as artists, the women's access to artistic education, career advancement in terms of getting equal opportunities, resources and recognition is a multifaceted issue to be critically assessed hence integrated into Gülsoy's novel as the author is consciously choosing real figures in order to address the power dynamics within art world and the society at large. In the same article, Shaw elaborates on the controversial nature of both the opportunities and the restrictions for the women as despite the growth of participation in the public sphere during the late Ottoman period, artistic practices were still subsumed within traditional gender roles (20–21).

Vasıf participates in the same competition anonymously but with a schematic, soulless, *didactique* painting (302) in his own outlook as he never shies away from self-criticism. "I even drew a woman picking fruit from a tree, I'm ashamed to describe it, for symbolism's sake…" (302). His artistic journey is not marked by a desire for grandiosity or too much attention unlike those who constantly whine about lack of appreciation or accredit failure to external factors. On the other side, Vasıf's first solo exhibition in 1958 featuring a wide range of works including sketches, paintings, mixed media pieces garners significant recognition only to be overshadowed by political crisis brought about by the revolution in the country which dramatically changes the priorities of the people. Despite experiencing a moment of fame as some of his works are bought by banks or collectors, the trajectory of art scene can be impacted with the politics and Gülsoy's fictionalization of such a detail is a testament to that.

Throughout the novel, Gülsoy makes it conspicuously felt that the art of storytelling is akin to the art of painting and for that reason probably Vasıf wants to be remembered most with the portrait he is drawing while narrating his story to the journalist Halit. Therefore, making a portrait is symbolic as the way he uses visual elements, colors in his composition is analogous to the ability of the writers using a descriptive language to evoke images in the readers' minds. For him, entitling different sections of his life in the book equals to finding a fitting name for a painting. While reflections of his early years, struggles and aspirations suggest a self-portrait of youth, explorations of love, loss, longing, family secrets, relationships haunt him like shadow of the past and his artistic journey catalyzes in the political upheavals which is accompanied by introspections and self-criticism.

Chapter 3
Painter's Rebellion by Gündüz Vassaf

Divided into four major parts, "Ortigia," "Lara," "On The Road" and "Procida," *Painter's Rebellion* intertwines realms of art and history through the protagonist's introspection into Caravaggio's life, many works and in particular *Burial of St. Lucy* (1608) which serves as the central thematic thread for the character who is enamored with it. The character's highly detailed visual journey which proceeds in accordance with Caravaggio's own journeys from Rome, Naples, Malta to Sicily, not only mirrors Caravaggio's unconventional approach to art, but it also turns into an individual journey of self-discovery as the character draws parallels between Caravaggio's time and his personal endeavors. Tracing Caravaggio's life, works and mysterious death becomes the point of reference for Gündüz Vasssaf in creating his novel as once again the storytelling is fused with the power of art.

The biography of Gündüz Vassaf reveals two crucial facts about the author who graduated from George Washington University with a degree in psychology, even developed Turkey's first intelligence tests, and at some point he was also teaching at Boğaziçi University which is actually before September 12 military coup. Both Vassaf and Gülsoy's works draw from various disciplines like psychology, philosophy, literature and art. Speaking of psychology, when asked about the character's relationship with Caravaggio and whether it is an obsession or not, Vassaf's response is quite clear and concise: "Rather than an obsession, it is identification."[9] That identification is not just for the nameless character who starts seeing himself in Caravaggio's life and works but Vassaf himself is the real figure who started this whole book project by looking at Caravaggio's paintings, taking notes and gradually putting himself in the artist's shoes especially in terms of the injustices he has been subjected to all his life. Therefore, the rebellion suggested in the title is twofold in the sense that Vassaf might have wished to endorse the artist's inequities and concurrently grant a voice so that his own arduousness can be heard.

Known for his characteristic application of light and shadow, Michelangelo Merisi da Caravaggio (1571–1610) is one of the most influential painters of Early Baroque Period. What makes Caravaggio appealing to the modern readers is also his compelling personality, "deviant sexuality, apparent atheism, and social transgressions" (Warwick 14) in that "he flaunted his originality; and mocked authority; he was fearless and belligerent, and in 1606 he killed a man, and spent his last years in exile" (Langdon 1). Of all the biographies on Caravaggio, Francine Prose provides the most interesting detail about the artist in that his birth actually occurs at an extraordinary moment in history as "Shakespeare's life

---

9   https://artdogistanbul.com/gunduz-vassaftan-bir-haksizlik-abidesi-olarak-caravaggio/

span, from 1564 to 1616, was remarkably close to Caravaggio's. And indeed an intensely Shakespearean spirit-theatrical, compassionate, alternately and simultaneously comic and tragic-suffuses Caravaggio's art…" (16–17). Reminiscent of that, at the beginning of the novel, Vassaf specifies the fact that, despite having left almost sixty works, fewer than Leonardo, Michelangelo, Van Gogh and Picasso, there are more books written on Caravaggio who lived both on the streets and in the palace judging by the fact that "his life and works were riven by a fracturing oscillation between high and low cultures: between the palace and the street, between knighthood and imprisonment, between painting and iconoclasm" (Warwick 15). He did what Shakespeare did in drama which is the empathy with characters. "His contemporaries are Marlowe who created modern drama, Monteverdi who invented opera and Cervantes, the father of novel" (Vassaf 33).

The popularity of Caravaggio owes a lot to the exhibition entitled "Mostra del Caravaggio e dei Caravaggeschi" organized by Roberto Longhi in 1951 and to a great extent, Thom Gunn's famous poem "In Santa Maria Del Popolo" which is an ekphrastic render on Caravaggio's *Conversion of St. Paul* (1600). The way Gunn first saw the painting in the church Santa Maria Del Popolo in Rome and was impressed to such an extent that he waited patiently an hour to see it in natural light as "the setting autumnal sun illuminated the shadowy and half-hidden Conversion" (Meyers 586) carries remarkable resonance with narrator/author who chronicles his first encounter as the novel becomes a textual counterpart to the actual painting. Meyers relates how "the mystical epiphany and harrowing conversion of Saul, the fanatical enemy of Christianity, and his transformation on the road to Damascus into the equally fanatical St. Paul, is one of the most famous incidents in religious history" (586) exploring themes of divine intervention, spiritual awakening and transformation. For the poet, the act of viewing this masterpiece also becomes a transformative experience akin to Saul in the painting. Such an awe, wonder and introspection becomes an impetus for Gunn to verbalize and meditate his experience in the form of a poem which becomes a vehicle of visual storytelling and artistic expression. Like Thom Gunn, Vassaf also responds to a visual art through literary expression, yet his approach and narrative scope go beyond capturing a single moment, personal and emotional insights. He also delves into historical, cultural and even psychological context allowing for a more comprehensive study while building an entire fiction through art and a specific visual stimulus.

A full appreciation of Caravaggio's indelible mark in history of art requires a particular understanding of his tumultuous life and unorthodox artistry that was marked by controversy, violence and legal troubles. The introductory notes of Francine Prose's *Caravaggio: Painter of Miracles* are striking:

> He was thirty-nine when he died, in the summer of 1610. He had been in exile, on the run, for the last four years of his life. He slept fully clothed, with his dagger by his side. He believed that his enemies were closing in on him and that they intended to kill him. He was wanted for murder in Rome, for stabbing a man in a duel that was said to have begun over a bet on a tennis game. It was not the first time that he had been in trouble with the law. He had been sued for libel, arrested for carrying a weapon without a license, prosecuted for tossing a plate of artichokes in a waiter's face, jailed repeatedly. He was accused of throwing stones at the police, insulting two women, harassing a former landlady, and wounding a prison guard. His contemporaries described him as mercurial, hot-tempered, violent. (1)

Caravaggio's personal life was dramatic and unprecedented yet profoundly canalized his artistic vision. As a means of maximizing the dramatic effect, using strong contrasts between light and dark, which is called *chiaroscuro*, is one of the defining features of Caravaggio's commitment to painting. Apart from bringing a different kind of realism and immediacy, his unconventional practices like using prostitutes, beggars or criminals as models challenge the idealized representations and in a sense, make religious narratives more relatable. One of the most notable examples of such paintings is *Burial of St. Lucy* which inaugurates the whole action and storyline in Vassaf's novel.

Burial of Saint Lucy

Painted in 1608 and located in the church of Santa Lucia al Sepolcro[10] in Syracuse, Sicily, *Burial of St. Lucy*, not only depicts a Christian martyr's burial but it also imbues a broader context of religious iconography as Caravaggio's typical mastery of composition offers meditation on faith, heavenly glory and explicates the precariousness of his personal circumstances at the time. The painting focuses on the funeral of Sicilian saint Lucy with the presence of a bishop, mourners and two muscular, gigantic gravediggers who almost dominate a quarter of the

---

10   According to Erin E. Hein's account, the church, occupies "a position of physical significance in Lucy's hagiography in the early modern period. It served as a monument that marked the exact location of her triumphal martyrdom and as a site for the perpetuation of her cult. Caravaggio's *Burial of Saint Lucy* was thus a culturally significant and site-specific commission for Santa Lucia al Sepolcro and the city of Siracusa, as it placed a visual simulacrum of Lucy's death and burial where the event originally occurred" (19).

canvas which is disproportionately divided between dark and light in line with Caravaggio's experiments with contrasting effects created through *chiaroscuro*. An important source on Caravaggio and the painting, *Caravaggio: A Passionate Life* by Desmond Seward remarks how Lucy, as the daughter of a wealthy, noble family, was "denounced as a Christian by the man to whom she was betrothed" (145). Refusing to be a sacrifice to the pagan gods, she is sentenced to death by a summoned crowd who miraculously cannot even move her let alone abuse her body until a sword is plunged into her throat. While looking at the death body of Lucy in the painting, Vassaf gives his account of the life story of the woman which might change in the religious doctrine it was recorded. The men are after Lucy of Syracuse who has a dowry worth of a fortune after losing her dad. He continues:

> In her dream, St. Agatha tells her that if she worships Jesus, her mother will be cured. With her wish granted, Lucia donates her virginity to Jesus, her fortune to the poor, and blinds herself so that her pursuer will leave her alone. Lamenting the loss of the dowry, the man denounces Lucia as a Christian. The Roman governor wants to send her to a brothel, but a thousand soldiers can't move the girl, who weighs like a stone. (102)

Ultimately Lucy endures tortures and before dying she is venerated as a saint for her faith in various Christian communions most notably in Catholic and Orthodox traditions. The boundary between the facts and lies is extensively blurred when it comes to unquestionable religious tenets as can be observed in the depiction of Lucy, as well. Caravaggio initially depicts Lucy with her head cut off in accordance with Catholic accounts which is against the Orthodoxes who say that a dagger was stuck in her throat. Vassaf notices that there is a slight scratch on her neck that can only be seen with a magnifying glass, probably as a means of pleasing both sides. What is so central to the etymology of the name "Lucy" is light and illumination as found in the root "lux." Being a saint capable of curing blindness and attracting pilgrims to the church where she is considered to have been martyred is still a point of obscurity. As indicated by Barbara Wisch in her work "St. Lucy in Text, Image, and Festive Culture" popular medieval book on saints' lives *Golden Legend* (1260–1265) makes no special mention of miracles of healing the blind but introduces her story (101). The narrator further contemplates:

> Although there is no mention in *The Golden Legend* of St. Lucy being blinded by her tormentors, as is sometimes claimed, another legend relates how, when a besotted admirer praised the beauty of her eyes excessively, she tore them out and gave them to him on a plate, whereupon they were miraculously restored to her. (146)

Regardless of the specific historical origins of Lucy's association with eyesight, her symbolism as a bearer of light and enlightenment has profound cultural and religious significance that can be traced in Caravaggio's masterpiece as well. Vassaf's ekphrastic rhetorical questions are also manifested in his occasional but repetitive references to *Burial of St. Lucy* as if it is fixed in his mind and all the narrative is built around it.

The character's observations on *Burial of St. Lucy* regarding the medley of visitors and their meditations feed into his personal reflections on the reasons why he keeps visiting the church every day and what changes it might cause him in the long run. He notices; the more he looks at the painting, the more he gets lost in his idiosyncratic thoughts and feels estranged mentally with such philosophical queries: "the more real something seems, the farther away it is from reality, the farther away it seems, the more real it is" (Vassaf 36). The character reminds the readers of an Ancient Greek story about painters Zeuxis and Parrhasius. Zeuxis creates such a realistic depiction of the grapes that, birds fly up to it to eat them. But more intriguingly, he loses the competition to Parrhasius when he asks him to lift the curtain so that he can look at his picture only to discover that the curtain is actually the painting. The legendary example highlights the pursuit of artistic excellence, rivalry and illusionistic techniques but more to the point, Zeuxis' ability in deceiving birds while Parrhasius' clever manipulation of fooling a fellow artist serves as a testament to associate birds with those regular visitors of Caravaggio's painting and the character with the one who is captivated to the point of illusion. Such dilemmas on reality and perception beckon the contradictory nature of representation in art implicating the discussions on imitation, mimesis.

The issue of authenticity is revived with an interesting story about Caravaggio's *Cardsharps* (1594), an early work from his career when he was not yet commissioned by the church. Vassaf draws attention to the details that Caravaggio dares to depict gambling in daily life in spite of Vatican prohibitions, creating a sensation for the Romans who were accustomed to religious paintings (54). On top of that, while using the same model for two young men, he once again deconstructs the conventions by depicting the innocent in the dark and the deceitful in the light. The position of the fingers of the man signaling or giving away the duplicities is the same as the pope's baptismal sign. He even claims that he makes us complicit as the silent viewers of that deception (54). Almost four hundred years later, a copy of *Cardsharps* is sold in Sotheby auction in 1965 only to be discovered to be authentic by the new owner who gets the painting tested with official ray lights. With the confirmation of other experts, the painting is valued at £11 million. Although the former owner files a lawsuit, the important thing is that it ignites the ongoing debate on the concept of authenticity in the world of painting (55). After all, Caravaggio, like many painters, is known for making multiple copies of his own paintings.

Death, Decapitation and Violence

According to Philip Sohm "death gives structure and meaning to Caravaggio's life" (449). Caravaggio's works elude easy interpretation but the themes of death, decapitation and violence can be seen as manifestations of his personal fears and anxieties given that he lived all his life in a constant fear of retribution which is marked in the following words:

> Because Caravaggio was a murderer, and because he often stabbed, battered, and molested, and because he populated his painted world with a high incidence, per capita, of beheadings and decapitated heads, biographers have seen violence and death as the central conceit of his life and art. (Sohm 450)

The intimate bond between Caravaggio's life and art is best manifested in the works encapsulating death and violence. In a sense, the dramatic contrast he introduced through *chiaroscuro* all mirrors the extremes of his life as violence, exile, legal troubles were imminent hence found a way into his paintings. According to John Berger, Caravaggio's chiaroscuro "reveals violence, suffering, longing, mortality..." (111). Although public decapitations and executions were so popular in Rome at the time, Caravaggio's interest in dark and violent pictures go beyond that. Thomas Puttfarken proposes a divergent standpoint suggesting "the treatment of violence is directly linked to that of naturalism, and the treatment of both to their treatment in painting" (186) which puts Caravaggio at the juncture of Aristotle's *Poetics* and Horace's *ut picture poesis*. The dramatic effect heightened by the essential feelings of fear and pity and the eventual cathartic emotions can be detected in Caravaggio's paintings as well. Caravaggio's combination of pictorial verisimilitude and violence might be as profound as the dramatic poetry hereby addressing the discussions of *paragone*. Contrary to existing views beholding painting as silent and static, Caravaggio's paintings in representation of violence achieve greater conviction.

In *David with the Head of Goliath* (1607) which is inspired by the Biblical story of David killing Philistine champion Goliath, Caravaggio focuses on the moment of victory in his depiction, yet unlike precedent version of the same narrative, Caravaggio portrays David in a detached, introspective mood instead of rejoicing at his triumph. Caravaggio treats a common subject in an unfamiliar way with a complicated, gentle expression on David's face. Graham-Dixon finds a different configuration in the portrayal of David and Goliath: "David evokes the youthful Christ, because the story of David slaying Goliath was often seen as an Old Testament prefiguration of Christ subduing Satan." (645). It is possible to find symbolic associations and parallelisms between David and Jesus Christ in terms of overcoming the evil and the dark in Christian contexts. Yet Vassaf brings another vivid interpretation in his repetitive question: "Does Caravaggio believe in what he painted? (59)" Contemplating that Caravaggio identifies with his characters and their dramas, Vassaf concludes that "he is both David and the giant Goliath that David slaughters" (59) perhaps prefiguring his own death. On the other hand, the story of David and Goliath falls in oedipal interpretation as in Freudian terms, decapitation equals to castration. Laura Schneider reminds that David is small, unarmed against the heavily armored Goliath and "this emphasis on the discrepancy in size between the two combatants is reminiscent of the small boy's perception of his father" (77).

"Decapitated heads" is a common theme in Caravaggio's paintings as afore-mentioned in David and Goliath. But the primary example is *Judith Beheading Holofernes* (1598) in which Caravaggio "neither censors nor embellishes violence" (119). According to Vassaf's contention this is the first anti-imperialist work of art history as Caravaggio evades both judgment and praise. In papal Rome, Caravaggio and many other Baroque artists rendered images of decapitated heads with blood gushing all over especially taking inspiration from Biblical stories like Judith that has been a subject of fascination for artists throughout history, inspiring numerous portrayals in various mediums. For Caravaggio's version, Vassaf gives a vivid visual depiction with ekphrastic resonances.

> Holofernes is on the bed with his naked body, his mouth open crying in terror, one hand clutching the sheet as if saying "Save me". His half-dead eyes bow to the inevitable while blood is gushing from his neck wound. Every fiber of her body is strained by this unexpected violence. Judith is a beauty that men can't take their eyes off. Her upturned nipples peeking out from her thin white blouse with low-cut lace embroidery, her up-turned skirt, her glittering earrings, her freshly done hair… Although she seems to be pulling herself away from the head she is cutting, she is tightly holding the gold-embroidered hunting knife in her hand. In the other hand, is the hair of Holofernes, which he pulled back to better slit his throat. Caravaggio's Judith says, "This is not for me, but I am still determined". (120)

Vassaf not only gives a visual representation invoking details in vividness through the use of language but he also adds depth by giving the depicted characters voice, making them speak which is in alliance with the rhetorical aspect of ekphrasis. Indeed, throughout history, there is a wide spectrum of Judith portrayals each reflecting a different aspect and interpretation.

> Baglione's half-naked, dull-faced Judith, is soon forgotten. Klimt portrays her as a Viennese bourgeois woman whose makeup looks running off her face. Cranach couldn't resist the demand; but all eight of his Judiths are as ordinary as postcard. Goya's Judith is resigned to her fate. (121)

Of all, Artemisia Gentileschi's depiction emphasizes a fierce woman who is even misandrist in her violent action. In an autobiographical manner, she focuses on Judith's merciless, undeterred expression as the painting becomes a means of redemption considering her personal infamy of rape and humiliation. Judith also marks a new period of drama and violence in his paintings that continued with *The Head of Medusa* which is located in Uffizi Gallery in Florence, *Beheading of St. John the Baptist* (1608), *Salome with the Head of John the Baptist* (1609), *Sacrifice of Isaac* (1603) and *David with the Head of Goliath* (1610). Charles Lewis underscores the change in the portrayals of beheading before and after Caravaggio himself kills a man in 1606 as oedipal conflicts and castration anxiety are evident in many of his works considering that his father also died only when he was six years old. What stands out in Lewis's article is the fact that while images of beheading prior to the murder, like Medusa or Judith, focus on the horror and pain, after the murder, "the victim is dead with lifeless eyes. Now the survivors struggle between the fascination of looking and not wanting to look, but are unable to walk away" (263). In a sense, following the crime Caravaggio wants to reenact the murderous act in an attempt of redemption.

Why Caravaggio?

Vassaf declares Caravaggio as the first psychologist of art history and gives another remarkable example from his oeuvre which is *The Musicians* (1595), located in Metropolitan Museum of Art in New York. The unorthodoxy of the painting can be sought in the iconography of the painting which features four boys whose faces reflect sadness, grief and even plea for help. As he never prefers to depict Jesus with his apostles and Mary in divine sanctity, Caravaggio skillfully veils sexual hunger as the commissioner Cardinal del Monte and his friends might have reveled at the maiden beauties of the boys in the painting (60). Vassaf even admits the inevitable similarities he finds in Caravaggio remembering the times he was an academic at Boğaziçi University. One day general secretary summons him to ask his whereabouts at night alleging that his nightlife is inappropriate for a university scholar (61). Caravaggio also lived in a difficult period of inquisitions and executions, when the Vatican dictated how paintings should be done. As the church had significant influence on arts, the artists were expected to adhere to strict rules and guidelines. While on one hand, he wanted to promote his paintings, he may have wanted to gain favor of the church and secure commissions. Therefore, even though he chose a style suiting Vatican propagandas, he actually managed to speak his own language such that he camouflages himself as a religious painter. Vassaf quotes from a modern media theorist, McLuhan who says, "the medium is the message" (61) in order to suggest how form and medium is important in conveying a message as in Caravaggio's case, his canvases serve as powerful means of communication especially in subtly subverting established norms.

The character bemoans about the fact that Caravaggio has always been judged and misapprehended even by famous thinkers and writers like Nicolas Poussin and John Ruskin which actually leads the factors in motivating Vassaf to create the novel as a means of redemption. The unnamed character/writer himself constantly refers to this undeniable and inevitable attraction to Caravaggio which also equals to giving voice to his own experiences and deep ties to his Turkish heritage. "He reminds me of my university years. The more I get to know him, the more I take a shine to him. We both started with full faith in our works, got halfway, became outcasts, and then villains. I didn't find intelligence in intelligence tests, neither did he find God in his religious paintings" (44). Comprehending and expounding Caravaggio's art is so complex that much needs to be said constructing a historical context especially in the seventeenth century Italian and European Art. Newly surfacing and evolving movements like Counter-Reformation, the renewal of the Roman Catholic Church against the spread of Protestantism, intersect with Caravaggio's art which had complex and controversial religious dynamics. Shockingly his art was mostly both in compliance and contradiction with such spirituality. A striking parallel is found in Turkish painter Osman Hamdi's provocative work *Mihrap* (1901) which proves that religious symbols cannot make a painter religious. "In the painting, the woman is sitting on the priest, with her back to the qibla. Her head is uncovered and her breasts are exposed. Under her feet are the Koran, the Zoroastrian Avesta and Buddhist books" (78). Hamdi's *Mihrap* also displays a bold statement in challenging religious dogmas as the woman's position which is the opposite direction of prayer in a mosque suggests a provocative commentary. For Vassaf another familiar figure that reminds him of Caravaggio and his years in Syracuse is Sultan Djem, son of Mehmed the Conqueror. All his life the Ottoman prince was also chased and imprisoned by knights who used him as a threat against Ottoman Empire and as a hostage whose presence brought advantage. Vassaf believes that "with the departure of Sultan Djem, who was also famous for his skills in poetry and painting, the Ottoman tendency towards Renaissance art came to an end" (80). Another similarity or identification that the character finds in Caravaggio is the date October 6. In 1608 Caravaggio escapes from prison of Sant'Angelo castle in Malta which was actually built against Ottoman attacks. On the same day the character leaves İstanbul accentuating the connection across time and space. While Caravaggio's route is Milan, Rome, Naples and Malta, his journey encapsulates Boston, Washington, Ankara and İstanbul.

Caravaggio's art has such a profound and transformative effect on Vassaf that it turns into a self-discovery and enrichment as he looks at the paintings, the more he researches about him, enters his world and travels along. Caravaggio's *Amor Victorious* (1602) and its homoerotic undertones provide broader exploration of sexuality in Caravaggio's work. The painting depicts Cupido, the god of love, as a naked boy with arrows in his hand, wings on his back, a mischievous smile, and a mocking gaze. As in many of his paintings, Caravaggio makes certain references to Michelangelo, his namesake.

> Caravaggio's "Amor Victorious" refers to Michelangelo's "The Rape of Ganymedes" in which Zeus takes the form of an eagle and kidnaps the most beautiful man on earth. Caravaggio depicts Michelangelo's idealized man as an ordinary man. By attaching Zeus' eagle wings to Cupido, he presents him in two roles, as both the attacker and the kidnapped man. (148)

Moreover, the interpretation extends beyond *Amor Victorious* to other works by Caravaggio such as *Boy with a Basket Fruit* (1593), *Musicians* (1595), *Bacchus* (1596) and his autobiographical painting *Young Sick Bacchus* (1593) which revolve around the same homoeroticism and might prompt speculations about Caravaggio's sexual orientation (148). The narrator discerns how his views on sexuality have also dramatically shifted in regards to making such elaborations on Caravaggio's paintings. He believes that because of his obsession of focusing on the beauty of women alone, he might be overlooking the beauty of men which also explains the initial repulsion he felt upon seeing the huge asses of grave diggers in *Burial of St. Lucy*. After all, the billboards or shop windows are decorated with tempting women's underwear not men's. In a sense by finding Cupido attractive, he notices that he can now evade sexual oppressions and concerns as the concept of beauty applies to men and women equally.

It is known that when Caravaggio arrived in Syracuse in 1608, he was on the run from the Maltese knights and law. In the book *Caravaggio: A Life Sacred and Profane*, Andrew Graham-Dixon mentions Caravaggio's friend and colleague Mario Minniti who welcomed him in his studio and helped for new commissions from the Senate which would also connote protection (394) and the genesis of new works like *Burial of St. Lucy*. The writer provides a highly physical depiction of the picture augmenting details and figures ranging from the gigantic gravediggers, the bishop and a group of mourners in the background who are staring down with grief at the dead body. What is prominently highlighted is the iconography of the picture which is "ingeniously suggestive of hope and redemption, but its mood is overwhelmingly bleak" (398). Despite the darkness in the mood, what cannot go unnoticed is the spatial link as Caravaggio also included a strong visual reference to the saint's original place of burial in his picture.

> The Church of Santa Lucia was built directly on top of the city's ancient Christian catacombs, where according to legend her body had first been put into the ground. The high, arched interior in which he set The Burial of St Lucy was directly based on those actual catacombs, which he had visited for himself; in this way, he perpetuated the act of interment linking Lucy to the city, creating an illusion that made it look as though her body was forever about to be entombed beneath the church itself. (399)

As the character continues visiting the church to see Lucy every day, he comes up with new discoveries and questions each day as his physical distance to the painting, daily light on the painting shift and give new perspectives to look at. He starts wondering about the people in the background assuming that Caravaggio might be sending a letter through the painting. He becomes particularly fixated on the obscured faces in the background, interpreting them as a deliberate act by Caravaggio to protect them from potential persecution by the Vatican as the figures could be the artists, poets, writers, dramatists of the time. The character's thoughts delve deeper into the symbolism of the painting, drawing connections between the burial of Lucy—named after Caravaggio's mother—and the concept of the death of God. He speculates whether Caravaggio intended the figures with shadowy faces to represent Jesus and his disciples, metaphorically burying a corrupted version of God, tainted by the influence of the Vatican. These musings lead the character down a path of philosophical inquiry, contemplating the role of religion, authority, and artistic expression in Caravaggio's time. In addressing religious issues in a controversial way or subverting the sacred, Vassaf draws comparisons between Caravaggio and Bruegel whose Jesus is lost in the crowd while people are engaged in daily, mundane business with complete indifference to others in *The Sermon of St. John the Baptist* (1566). He thinks about how he was unable to find the saint in the painting when he first saw it. Perplexingly, in the foreground is a gypsy reading the fortune of a man while St. John, with his brown broadcloth is in the background, barely visible. Bruegel is also visually echoing the pressure of Vatican, given that in Bruegel's time, out of fear of the Inquisition, Protestant priests would meet secretly with their followers far from the city and rage against the Pope. As in many of his painting such as *The Suicide of Saul, The Census at Bethlehem, The Procession to Calvary* and *Conversion of St. Paul,* Jesus is a tiny figure, the size of an ant that no-one recognizes.

The Beheading of St. John the Baptist (1608), located in Malta, is the last painting Caravaggio paints before having been forced to escape to Syracuse. The painting, located in the oratory of Co-Cathedral of St. John in Valletta, is a massive altarpiece, actually his largest work, measuring almost twelve feet tall. Francine Prose remarks unlike his previous works "in which the worst is about to occur, this painting is set at the moment in which it already has" (129). Besides, St. John's tragedy is not over yet as the blood is streaming from his neck, the executioner's hand is reaching behind for the dagger while the other hand is grabbing his hair so that he can complete the decapitation. According to the Graham-Dixon:

> The story of St John's martyrdom is told in the New Testament books of Matthew (14:3–12) and Mark (6:17–28). King Herod had thrown John into prison because he had dared to reprimand him for his illicit marriage to Herodias. Herod's consort plotted with her daughter, Salome, to bring about John's execution. At the king's birthday feast, Salome danced so seductively for Herod that he granted her anything she desired. She asked for the head of John the Baptist. An executioner beheaded the saint in his prison. The severed head was laid on a platter and given to Salome at the feast. (730–31)

St. John the Baptist is also considered to be "the knights' protector in the holy land, on Rhodes and on Malta" (Seward 131) as everyone believed that the Ottomans had abandoned the Great Siege on the day the Baptist was seen in the clouds coming to their rescue in 1565, leaving the knights eventually victorious (131). Therefore, no other subject would have better impact on Maltese knights since there are sources holding the idea that the executioner or the man standing next to him with keys in his hand directing the whole operation, could be a Turk which is point emphasized by Vassaf, as well (183). The painting is also one of the few paintings Caravaggio signed with "F. Michelangelo" probably referring to his knighthood:

> It stands for 'Fra', or 'Brother', the official prefix of any Knight of St John.63 The artist's signature, written in John the Baptist's blood, was a public proclamation. It was Caravaggio's way of asserting that his own mortal sin, the murderous letting of a man's blood, had been washed away by the blood of his new patron saint. Now he could return to Rome, not as a criminal but as a proud Christian soldier. (Graham-Dixon 736)

At the time, Caravaggio's arrival in Malta, as a celebrated painter, is highly newsworthy since despite the Pope's death warrant, the fact that he receives the title of "Cavaliere di Obbedienza" paves the way for him to be welcomed on the island and even be allowed to paint for European palaces. The fact that he was bestowed with two Turkish slaves as part of his knighthood adds an intriguing layer to his story, especially considering the presence of Turkish imagery in some of his paintings. The speculation is also raised by Vassaf who questions whether the officer overseeing the execution in his St. John the Baptist painting was wearing Ottoman clothes or whether the two gravediggers in *Burial of St. Lucy*, the first painting he painted in Sicily after his escape, were these two Turkish slaves. Yet such a high note in his career and reputation last very briefly with his abrupt fall from grace and arrest (215). Although there is no document about his imprisonment, what is certain is that he escaped in 1608 after fifteen months in Malta which marks another chapter in his tumultuous life.

Tracing Caravaggio in Paris, London, Florence and Rome

In the second part of the novel which is entitled "Lara," even though the character moves away from his passion for Caravaggio because of his love for Lara, he sets out to meet a writer who believes that Caravaggio is buried on the island of Procida in the Gulf of Naples, thus giving the readers preliminary information about the subsequent parts of the novel, "On the Road" and "Procida." Before undergoing an eye operation, the unnamed character decides to visit Louvre Museum to view Caravaggio's three paintings there, *Death of the Virgin* (c. 1601–1606), *Fortune Teller* (1597) and *Portrait of Alof de Wignacourt and his Pageboy* (c. 1607–1608). At this point, the author mentions a place close to where he stays in Paris and numerous Turkish poets, artists and writers he meets there. He makes a reference to Turkish poet-painter Nazım Hikmet whose family struggles to survive penniless while the poet's books are "monopolized by the rich publishing houses in Turkey" (491) shedding light on the socio-economic challenges faced by many artists and intellectuals. Nazım Hikmet becomes another pivotal figure that Vassaf draws analogy with Caravaggio as he also lived his life under threat, faced persecution for his beliefs, was declared as an enemy by the state for his ideology and eventually imprisoned yet his poems continued to resonate even to the point of being used for political rallies. Moreover, since France and the Louvre Museum are identified with Leonardo da Vinci's Mona Lisa, Nazım Hikmet's famous lines come to mind taken from his long poem entitled "Jokond and Si-Ya-U" in which the Chinese Si-Ya-U whom the poet encountered in real life during his time in Moscow is a persistent visitor of Mona Lisa at Louvre Museum. Through such an imaginative fusion, the poet not only gives voice and movement to the painting, he also gradually questions the phenomenon of the museum denying the sanctity of museums, so to speak, by alluding to the boredom of it. Vassaf narrates how Nazım Hikmet makes Mona Lisa speak:

It is good to visit a museum
But not be a museum piece
I was put in this palace that imprisons past
With such severe judgement
While my face cracks out of boredom
I wish
Leonardo da Vinci's bones be a brush for a cubist painter
As he put this cursed smile in my mouth
Like a gold-plated tooth
With his painted hands around my throat… (493–494)

When it comes to Caravaggio paintings at Louvre, Vassaf specifies *Death of the Virgin*, another controversial work from his oeuvre. Vassaf mentions that the model in the painting, lying on the bed with her bare feet and red dress, is Caravaggio's lover Lena Antognetti, who committed suicide (495). The interpretations made by some art historians on the issue of religious allegory in the painting with the bare feet symbolizing faith, her red dress representing resurrection after death, and the swollen belly signifying virtue contrasts with the scandalous reception in Rome. "Never before in the history of Christian painting had Mary, mother of Gold, been made to seem as and frail and vulnerable as this" (Graham-Dixon 606). Once again Caravaggio challenges the conventional idealization of Mary as ethereal, giving her a lifeless scene surrounded by apostles. Although the painting was intended for The Church of Santa Maria della Scala, it was soon rejected and removed with the further speculations that his Madonna was modeled on a prostitute.

The second painting he gazes upon is *The Portrait of Alof de Wignacourt* which is another painting Caravaggio made during his time in Malta in order to be knighted. According to Vassaf's perspective, instead of capturing the commanding presence and authority of Grand Master who is particularly known for his role defending Malta against external threats, like Ottoman siege, Caravaggio might be exposing the sodomy of the old man in heavy armor as the attention is also put on the pageboy who is sarcastically beaming. It is possible to assume that in securing the knighthood Caravaggio not only made use of his strong connections, patrons in Rome but also the favor he gained through this portrait. Francine Prose asks similar questions like why the little servant is in the painting at all or what his relation to the older man is (127–128). Still, rather than presenting a traditional military portrait which would be an unexpected, extremely unfamiliar effort by Caravaggio, he preserves the aura of enigma by rendering such subtle gestures, elements of secrecy as the artist's ability lies in withholding as much as revealing.

The character's ultimate desire to see Caravaggio's paintings before his surgery drags him from Paris to London, to the National Gallery, where three of Caravaggio's paintings are housed; *Boy Bitten by a Lizard* (1593–1594), *Supper at Emmaus* (1601) and *Salome with the Head of St. John the Baptist* (1607) and finally to Rome which was at the time of Caravaggio a city of migration. "Its shifting population was drawn from every corner of the Christian world—priests seeking preferment, pilgrims seeking salvation, courtesans seeking riches." (Graham-Dixon 156). In Rome, the character ponders on the figure of Christ in Caravaggio's paintings, which is eleven in total according to his account, and why art historians never inquiries into the model he used as each painting portrays a different Jesus. 1590s Rome was a city of ruthless suppressions rather than creative imaginative compositions. A pivotal figure from this period Giordano Bruno "who believed in a thousand different worlds spinning through space, but denied the existence of God—was burned at the stake in 1600" (Graham-Dixon 162) arouses interest in the character who disparately infers that Bruno might be Jesus in Caravaggio's paintings. Bruno's execution serves as a reminder of the consequences and harsh punishment of dissent. Although artists at the time were expected to conform to established norms, Caravaggio's bold approach and challenges to restrictions would corroborate such an assertion. While trying to give Caravaggio the recognition he deserves through his novel, Vassaf remembers Bruno as well, as the readers can access a petition calling on Vatican and Pope to restore Giordano Bruno's reputation through a QR code at the end of the book.

In Rome the character's road map is completely based on the churches in which Caravaggio paintings are located. *Madonna of Loreto* (1604) at Basilica of St. Augustine, *The Conversion of Saul* (1600) at Santa Maria del Popolo, *The Calling of Saint Matthew* (1600), *The Martyrdom of St. Matthew* (1600), and *The Inspiration of Saint Matthew* (1602) at San Luigi dei Francesi, the Contareli Chapel are the destinations to visit. In particular, the paintings on the biblical narratives of St. Matthew picturing St. Matthew being called by Jesus, writing the Gospel and being martyred in Africa deviate from religious iconographical traditions. As its title suggests, *The Calling St. Matthew* focus on the moment Matthew, a tax collector was called by Jesus to become one of his disciples. Caravaggio's unconventional approach comes from the setting he chooses as it diverges from idealized biblical scenes; "a dingy room somewhere in modern Rome" (Graham-Dixon 390) or "Taverna di Turco" (538) in Vassaf's words, or according to Prose, he brings "the scared down from the realm of the eternal and the ethereal into the temporal and earthly" (66). Recalling the scene in *Cardsharps*, Matthew and his companions are astonished at Jesus' command to follow him. The second of the canvases at the chapel, *The Martyrdom of St. Matthew* highlights how he was killed in Ethiopia after converting many people to Christianity and even establishing a church. Dramatically, as Vassaf also marks while the saint is writhing helplessly on the ground, the killer to behead him is at the center of the painting with his naked torso reminiscent of ancient Greek heroes (539).

Before the final part which is about the character's tracking where Caravaggio was buried, he goes to Florence as the last city to see some of his paintings hanging in the Pitti Palace, like *The Sleeping Cupid* (1608) and *Portrait of Far Antonio Martelli* (1608), a distinguished knight of Malta who gained recognition during the Great Siege against the Turks. *The Sleeping Cupid* also offers a departure from classic portrayals in that Cupid "looks more like a dead baby" (Seward 134), "fat, puffy-faced, ugly and passed out from alcohol" (Vassaf 567). Two more notable paintings housed at Uffizi are *Bacchus* (1595) and *Medusa* (1597) and accordingly in an iconographical and ekphrastic manner, Vassaf points out what is obvious. As the god of wine, revelry, fertility and drama from Roman mythology, Bacchus, with his half naked body, a crown of grape-leaves on his head, offers another enigmatic, bold portrayal. The composition includes various symbolic elements, such as the pomegranates with their seeds bursting from the fruit basket, representing fertility, and the rotten apple, symbolizing the transience of life. For Vassaf the painting projects the private lives of the nobles at a time when homoerotic relationships were crime, yet the fact that it is a self-portrait, might be granting a sort of immunity for the artist (571).

While exploring the themes of sensuality and lust with bold artistic approaches and undertones, Caravaggio navigates between the realms of divinity and profane, the earthly human experience. Caravaggio's *Medusa* which is painted on a shield, captures the dramatic moment of a famous mythological scene in which snake-haired Medusa who was capable of turning people into stone with her petrifying gaze, shows her slayed head with wide open eyes and screaming mouth. As decapitation, severed heads is so often figured in Caravaggio's paintings, Vassaf believes that Caravaggio must have identified with Medusa commenting that it is "an expression of rebellion against injustice" (571). Another theme rooted in the image is suggested by Nikčević who considers that "the painting was likely produced in the manner of a self-portrait rendered with the use of a convex mirror" (81). The writer hits the right notes in his contention as Medusa is the only non-religious decapitation in the artist's oeuvre and it was made in 1597 which precedes the murder he committed. Incorporating his own likeness into images for certain figures in his paintings is an artistic convention found in many of Caravaggio woks as he also did in the decapitated head of Goliath. In the case of Medusa, placing himself in the terrifying facial expression of a female mythological figure could inevitably be linked with castration fear as looking through Freudian lens has become an interpretive reflex underscoring the artist's presumed homosexuality and unresolved oedipal conflicts. On the other hand, Caravaggio's decision to paint the image on a convex shield not only references mythological symbolism but also a distinctive virtuosity.

> Medusa's appearance upon Caravaggio's shield suggests another implication or connotation of the image. For we recall that Perseus, who slayed Medusa by cutting off her head, survived her deadly gaze by looking not directly upon her, but at her reflection on his shield. Caravaggio's image thus evokes the very shield of Perseus, in which case we, in the place of Perseus, gaze upon a lifesaving reflection. (Barolsky 28)

In that way Caravaggio's Medusa turns the viewers, onlookers into stone to the point of stunning them with such virtuosity in a two dimensional medium blurring the line between the real and the represented image. These paintings suggest a complex interplay between artistic expressions and psychoanalytic symbolism going beyond mere aesthetic appeal for both the viewers and Caravaggio himself.

Who Killed Caravaggio?

The character's departure from Rome takes him to a train route that includes stops at Naples, Messina, Taormina, Catania and finally Syracuse. As the train stops for two hours in Messina, a northern Sicilian town, the character finds the opportunity to visit Museo Regionale which has *The Adoration of Shepherds* and *The Raising of Lazarus*, two commissions Caravaggio received in 1608–1609. Of the two, Lazarus is more attractive for Vassaf as *The Adoration of Shepherds* is another non-classic religious painting, deprived of typical Christian iconography. Yet the story of Lazarus is rarely depicted and according to many biographers and anecdotes of Sussinno, as Vassaf also makes use of in his narration, Caravaggio used a hospital room and a real corpse in pursuit of indeterminate naturalistic manner and even attacked the models who refused to pose holding a corpse and complained about the smell. Painted in honor of Lazzari family, the story embedded in the paintings is cited in the following account provided by Andrew Graham-Dixon:

> The parable of Lazarus was traditionally regarded as a miracle performed by Christ in prefiguration of his own crucifixion. In raising Lazarus from the tomb, Christ saved him from sin and death, just as by dying on the Cross, he would save mankind from Original Sin and open the way to salvation. Caravaggio was certainly aware of the theological parallel, since he has arranged Lazarus's body in the same configuration as that of Christ on the Cross. Lazarus's two sisters, Martha and Mary, gather around him like the mourners of Christ at the moment of his deposition. (785–786)

Reminding of *Burial of St. Lucy*, Caravaggio paints a scene of death, darkness, desperation and people gathered around probably recalling his childhood memories in Milan. What leads Caravaggio to leave Messina is an interesting allegation that he was watching young male students at a local school which was suspiciously questioned by the schoolmaster and ultimately ended in an incident of temper and rage for Caravaggio. While the character's obsession with Caravaggio and his art encompasses the first three parts, he continues his journey in Procida seeking after his death as the speculations surrounding Caravaggio's death are as enigmatic and uncertain as his life and works.

Remarkable archival and biographical studies most notably supplemented by Giovanni Baglione (1642) and Giovan Pietro Bellori (1672), extend the factual information about his life and artistry but different theories on his death also garner a plethora of interpretations. Such diversity and complexity could be evaluated as the genesis and impulsion of Vassaf's novel through fictionalizing, blending and integrating into his own life. For that reason, towards the end of the novel, the character's search and pursuit of Caravaggio culminates in Procida, an island nearby Naples. Although his final years are also marked with turmoil and legal troubles, he continues his artistic productivity some of which are also visited by the character. Among them, *The Flagellation of Christ* (1607), one of the Neapolitan altarpieces is exhibited at Museo di Capodimonte today despite being commissioned for a chapel in the church of San Domenico Maggiore. The character distinguishes how the attention is put on the flagellant in the painting rather than the pain and suffering of Jesus. He asks "who is Caravaggio writing a letter to with the sadistic happiness of the flagellant instead of emphasizing the pain of Jesus?" (629). In a contrasting manner with earlier depictions, Caravaggio places the focus on the Roman soldiers. As Caravaggio's life was marked by exile and displacement, themes like flagellation which is deeply rooted in religious iconography provides him with focal points or poignant moments for spiritual contemplation. Yet his interpretation goes beyond classic, orthodox imagery as Caravaggio's intention of fostering a sense of connection to the suffering and torment of Jesus raises doubt and uncertainty for the character as well. The sort of image for similar religious veneration with unconventional depiction is carried on in *The Seven Acts of Mercy* (1607) as "the painting seems chaotic, almost circus like, and unfocused" (Prose 118). The painting is the first masterpiece Caravaggio makes after killing a man and fleeing Rome. His arrival in Naples in 1606 is followed with prestigious commissions including this particular painting that was intended for the church of a charitable organization need Pio Monte della Misericordia. The seven works or acts of corporal mercy in Christianity are visiting the imprisoned, feeding the hungry, burying the dead, sheltering the homeless, clothing the naked, caring for the sick and refreshing the thirsty which are all composed in the bottom half of the painting while in the upper part, Mary, her baby Jesus and winged angels are looming in the air, watching the chaos in the earthly realm. Vassaf interprets this stark contrast as bringing the street into the church as if to hold a mirror to the double standards of the rich (633). Ralf van Bühren arises the same point asking "Why do the heavenly company not interfere in the earthly proceedings?" (77). It is hard to rule out the possibility that Caravaggio, who was in desperate need of mercy himself, had the inner chaos of desiring pardon amidst earthly struggles. Rendering such a painting might be a heavenly manifestation but his personal matters and how alienated he feels is no different than the remote observation of heavenly figures to the suffering of those below.

The character's exploration of Caravaggio ends in Naples to see *The Marytrdom of St. Ursula* (1610) which is thought be the artist's last painting. The painting depicts the moment Atilla, Hun leader who conquered Europe, killing Ursula with his arrow: "The story of the gruesome martyrdom that it depicts comes from *The Golden Legend*, which tells how the virgin Ursula was murdered by a king of the Huns for refusing to marry him, and how he shot her with an arrow" (Seward 162). It is such a scene that the killer and the victim both look shocked and detached. Caravaggio captures the saint's fixed gaze on her wound trying to understand what happened but at the same time reflecting a spiritual resolve. The character continues to find a personal connection with Caravaggio's works saying: "I saw Lara and me in their faces, in their submissions to the roles Vatican fairy tale had assigned their fates with" (658). Because in the days of Procida, the character receives a letter before Lara and suddenly finds her at his doorstep. Lara, who says she is pregnant, turns out to be depressed and has pregnancy delusions such as belly swelling, milk coming from breasts or feeling the baby's movements. Graham-Dixon claims that the saint as the victim of a sexual insult "responds by subjecting the woman who had scorned him to a vile parody of pregnancy" (818). The painted saint has a swollen belly which is pierced through the arrow, metaphorically giving birth to her death as the blood is spurting. Ironically Lara, who was a sexual assault victim as a child, hopes to start a new life after discovering and embracing the truth about her non-existent pregnancy. After executing this painting, Caravaggio leaves Naples, still hoping a pardon from Pope for the murder he had committed but tragically dies without making it to Rome. As there are still various, unanswered theories regarding Caravaggio's untimely death, the character also ponders on the repeated questions who killed Caravaggio or how he died. Many sources capitalize on Baglione's telling which reports that Caravaggio is mistakenly arrested after going ashore. After a two-day imprisonment, he is released but gets furious upon finding out that the *felucca* left without him. Finally, having lost all his belongings, he becomes so sick in July heat that, in Porto Ercole he dies within a few days "miserably-indeed, just as he had lived" (Friedlaender 236) which is an account the character also seems to agree with.

Caravaggio's life and art is so captivating that, the dichotomy between his troublemaker image and artistic genius does not shy large crowds away from going after his legacy which is the impetus for the character in the novel as well. Unlike his predecessors and contemporaries, Caravaggio refuses to conform to the idealized representations and societal structures. Occasionally he gets support of some cardinal names but his groundbreaking approach to art does not inexorably strive for acceptance in favorable environments. Those who emulate his artistic legacy are not just Italians as his impact extend to the rest of world which ultimately leads to the emergence of what is known as Caravaggisti. With his novel, Vassaf as the narrator/author/character creates an introspective and expansive narrative delving into historical, cultural, artistic and psychological contexts hence turning his undeniable attraction into an identification and ultimately a redemption.

Concluding Remarks

This book seeks to elaborate on the legacy and evolution of coalescence of art and literature in Turkey from a historical and cultural threshold while introducing complementary analysis of two novels by contemporary Turkish writers; Murat Gülsoy's *Painter Vasıf's History of Secret Loves* and Gündüz Vassaf's *Painter's Rebellion*. The engagement with the interplay between art and writing, how art enhances critical thinking and writing skills, inspiring characters, plots culminates in both novels which craft visual narratives. Both writers use the same fictionalization technique which is based on meticulous, documentary research as while Gülsoy gathers a great deal of information on the history of modern Turkish painting through real figures, Vassaf garners a wealth of information on Caravaggio's life, oeuvre, final years and death with a similar historical accuracy.

Composed of different sub-sections, the first part of the book traces the emergence of art and shamanism which is intricately and concurrently linked in the early cave paintings, drawings and the tradition of painting in Turkish records, like the Gokturk Inscriptions and the changing artistic traditions with the adoption of different religions like Manichaeism, Buddhism in the Uighurs and Islam in the Ottoman Period. As an important artistic heritage in Islamic culture, the art of miniature painting which developed under Ottoman patronage not only decorated books intricately interweaving poetry with the painting, merging the visual with the literary with its own distinctive style disregarding perspective, anatomy, light and shadow but also emphasized detailed ornamentation enhancing the aesthetic appeal and narrative illustration depicting scenes from history, literature and life. Accordingly, Orhan Pamuk's *My Name is Red* as an exemplary work with its subject matter and narrative style is elucidated to examine the consequences of the prohibition on the art of painting, its ensuing effects and the hybridity of Eastern image with Western discourse which is found in the art of miniature. The transition to European art trends and the emergence of new forms aligning with modern aesthetics witnessed an exposure to Western ideas and movements initiating the tradition of visual arts-poetry or painting-poetry led by Tevfik Fikret, Nazım Hikmet, Bedri Rahmi Eyüboğlu, Ilhan Berk, Oktay Rifat whose works converge visual and poetic elements. This preliminary part frames how the relationship between visual arts and literature has brought different approaches throughout the ages with deep historical roots and offers a foregrounding data to embark on journeys through the narratives within visual creativity.

In his novel *Painter Vasıf's History of Secret Loves*, Murat Gülsoy highlights the interconnectedness of visual and literary art forms in his documentary novel with his unique approach to art and in particular creative writing showcasing a deep engagement with the intricacies of the human mind and the creative process.

The novel's journey from Paris to Istanbul connecting the historical transformation of modern Turkish painting reflects a fusion of fictional and the real as the fictitious protagonist Vasıf and historical figures generate a narrative that is both imaginative and rooted in concrete reality. Gündüz Vassaf's lengthy novel *The Painter's Rebellion* also presents an exploration of art and history blending genres like fiction, memoir and biography in four major parts; "Ortigia," "Lara," "On the Road" and "Procida." Caravaggio's life and art intertwine with conflicts, imprisonment, violence and death as the artist was constantly on the move following the murderous incident in Rome, and was forced to travel to various cities including Malta, Sicily and Naples. The character's introspection into Caravaggio's life and one particular painting, *Burial of St. Lucy*, not only gives insight into the painter's unconventional approach to art challenging established norms, but the thematic resonances between Caravaggio's paintings, life and the time period he lived and the protagonist's own life and the contemporary issues in Turkey suggest a further consideration on the role of art in constructing an entire fiction around the idea of it.

For both novels, visuals play such a crucial role that, both authors take advantage of technological novelties in order to engage readers; Gülsoy employs artificial intelligence to prepare an exhibition catalog for his fictional painter protagonist while Vassaf incorporates QR codes to provide access to Caravaggio's paintings, a petition for Giordano Bruno, another convicted artist, and a music selection he listened to writing the novel. Gülsoy fictionalizes an imaginary painter by embedding him among real events and people but provides a critical view of the periods in Vasıf's lifetime which politically, historically and culturally mirror the evolution of art and literature in Turkey. On the other side, the unnamed character's obsession with Caravaggio, a real painter, his life, art, works and death becomes an identification and personal quest transforming into an artistic process. Such that the line between the narrating character and the author is blurred, ultimately giving Caravaggio in whom the character finds so much of himself, a voice of rebellion across centuries.

To conclude, the evocative power of visual arts in sparking reflective writing is crucial in these novels as artworks, in particular paintings, can provide a diverse range of stimuli. Both novels suggest a broader contemplation of the role of art in constructing a narrative which is an important appeal in international literary sphere. As the longstanding relationship between painting and poetry, which is marked by either rivalry or parity throughout history, is deeply rooted in a shared interest of artistic expressions in different domains—visual or literary—it becomes transparent that convergence between art and literature highlights a collaborative potential in affirming a timeless, universal bond.

Works Cited

Ağıl, Nazmi. *Ekphrasis: Turkey and the West*. Simurg, 2016.

Akşehir, Mahinur. "Murat Gülsoy Critical Biography." *DLB 379: Turkish Novelist, Second Series (Dictionary of Literary Biography, 379)*, edited by Burcu Alkan and Çimen Erkol Günay. Gale Cenage Learning, 2017, pp. 119–128.

Anar, Turgay. "Nazım Hikmet Şiirinde Ekfrasis." *Selçuk Üniversitesi Türkiyat Araştırmaları Dergisi*, vol. 53, 2021, pp. 137–162. https://doi.org/10.21563/sutad.1052251

Barolsky, Paul. "The Ambiguity of Caravaggio's 'Medusa.'" *Source: Notes in the History of Art*, vol. 32, no. 3, 2013, pp. 28–29. *JSTOR*, http://www.jstor.org/stable/23392422.

Baysal, Abidin Müslüm. "D Grubu'nun Türk Resim Sanatında Özgünlük Açısından Önemi." *Ankara Üniversitesi Güzel Sanatlar Fakültesi Dergisi*, vol. 3, no. 1, 2021, pp. 29–45.

Berger, John. *Portreler*. Translated by Beril Eyüboğlu. Metis Yayınları, 2018.

Biçer Özcan, Şehnaz. "Uygur Minyatürlerinde Metin-Resim İlişkisi ve Sonrası." *İstem*, vol. 3, 2018, pp. 125–145. https://doi.org/10.31591/istem.426435.

Binark, İsmet. "Türkler'de Resim ve Minyatür Sanatı." *Vakıflar Dergisi*, vol. 12, 1978, pp. 271–289.

Boyle, John Andrew. "Turkish and Mongol Shamanism in the Middle Ages." *Folklore*, vol. 83, no. 3, 1972, pp. 177–193. *JSTOR*, http://www.jstor.org/stable/1259544.

Bühren, Ralf van. "Caravaggio's 'Seven Works of Mercy' in Naples: The Relevance of Art History to Cultural Journalism." *Church, Communication and Culture*, vol. 2, no. 1, 2017, pp. 63–87. https://doi.org/10.1080/23753234.2017.1287283.

Burnett, Ron. *How Images Think*. The MIT Press, 2004.

Cecan, Besi. *Düğün: Şiir—Resim—Heykel*. Mas Matbaacılık, 2014.

Çete, Şilan. "Gündüz Vassaf'tan bir Haksızlık Abidesi olarak Caravaggio" *Art Dog İstanbul: Contemporary Deductions*, August 8, 2023. https://artdogistanbul.com/gunduz-vassaftan-bir-haksizlik-abidesi-olarak-caravaggio/

Ekici, Ayşe. *Sanatlararası Etkileşim Bağlamında Resim ve Şiir İlişkisi*. 2019. Anadolu Üniversitesi, MA dissertation.

Ercivan Zencirci, Dizar, Ebru Kabakçı and Köseoğlu Kamuran. "Şiirden Baskı Resme Yansımalar'ın Ekfraktik İncelemesi." *İdil,* vol. 103, 2023, pp. 292–305. https://doi.org/10.7816/idil-12-103-02.

Ergin, Muharrem. *Orhun Abideleri*. Hisar Kültür Gönüllüleri, 2003.

Ezik, Abdullah. "Murat Gülsoy: 'Elbette Gayriresmî, Oldukça Öznel Bir Tarih Anlatısı Bu." *Sanat Kritik Birlikte Okumak Yazmak ve Düşünmek İçin…*,

January 24, 2023. https://sanatkritik.com/soylesi/murat-gulsoy-elbette-gay riresmi-oldukca-oznel-bir-tarih-anlatisi-bu/

Fırat, Özden Begüm. *Encounters with the Ottoman Miniature: Contemporary Readings of an Imperial Art.* I. B. Tauris, 2015.

Friedlaender, William. *Caravaggio Studies.* Princeton University Press, 1974.

Genç, Mehmet Ali. "D Grubu Ressamlarının Türk Resim Sanatının Gelişimine Olan Katkıları." *Idil Sanat ve Dil Dergisi,* vol. 1, 2012. https://doi.org/10.7816/idil-01-05-27.

Gombrich, E. H. *The Story of Art.* Phaidon Press, 1995.

Gombrich, E. H. *Art and Illusion: A Study in the Psychology of Pictorial Representation.* Princeton University Press, 2000.

Graham-Dixon, Andrew. *Caravaggio: A Life Sacred and Profane,* W. W. Norton & Company, 2011.

Gülsoy, Murat. *Büyübozumu Yaratıcı Yazarlık: Kurmacanın Bilinen Sırları ve İhlal Edilebilir Kuralları.* Can Yayınları, 2004.

Gülsoy, Murat. *Ressam Vasıf'ın Gizli Aşklar Tarihi.* Can Yayınları, 2023.

Halman, Talat S. *A Millenium of Turkish Literature: A Concise History.* Ed. Jayne L. Warner. Syracuse University Press, 2011.

Hein, Erin. "Making a Martyr: Preserving and Creating Cultural Identity through Caravaggio's *Burial of Saint Lucy* (1608)." *Athanor,* vol. 36, 2018, pp. 19–26.

Kavcar, C. "Tevfik Fikret ve Güzel Sanatlar." *Ankara University Journal of Faculty of Educational Sciences (JFES),* vol. 15, no. 2, 2019, pp. 131–150. https://doi.org/10.1501/Egifak_0000000906.

Kaya, Nilay. *Evliyâ Çelebi'nin Seyahatnâmesi'nde Görsel Sanat Eserlerinin Tasviri: Ekfrastik Bir Yaklaşım.* 2016. Bilkent University, Ph.D. dissertation.

Kırca, Mustafa. "(Western)Word/(Eastern)Image in My Name is Red: An Imagological Reading of Orhan Pamuk's Ekphrastic Reimagination." *Ordu Üniversitesi Sosyal Bilimler Enstitüsü Sosyal Bilimler Araştırmaları Dergisi,* vol. 12, no. 1, 2022, pp. 33–42. https://doi.org/10.48146/odusobiad.1039162.

Koç, Malike Bileydi. "Türk Resim Tarihinde Askeri Ressamlar Dönemi Ve Bahriyeli Ressam İsmail Hakkı Bey." *Marmara Türkiyat Araştırmaları Dergisi,* vol. 9, no. 2, 2022, pp. 169–201. https://doi.org/10.16985/mtad.1102283.

Köker, Saniye. "Murat Gülsoy'un Tanrı Beni Görüyor mu? Adlı Kitabında Fotoğraf-Öykü İlişkisi." *Erciyes Akademi,* vol. 36, no. 4, 2022, pp. 1940–1956. https://doi.org/10.48070/erciyesakademi.1160119.

Krauth, Nigel and Christopher Bowman. "Ekphrasis and the Writing Process." *New Writing,* vol. 15, no. 1, 2018, pp. 11–30. https://doi.org/10.1080/14790726.2017.1317277.

Langdon, Helen. *Caravaggio: A Life*. Pimlico, 1999.

Lewis, Charles N. "Caravaggio's Imagery of Death and Allusion." *American Imago*, vol. 43, no. 3, 1986, pp. 261–272. *JSTOR*, http://www.jstor.org/stable/26304005.

Meyers, Jeffrey. "Thom Gunn and Caravaggio's *Conversion of St. Paul*." *Style*, vol. 44, no. 4, 2010, pp. 586–590. *JSTOR*, http://www.jstor.org/stable/10.5325/style.44.4.586. Accessed March 6, 2024.

Michaelson, Susan. "The Hand on the Wall of the Cave: Exploring Connections between Shamanism and the Visual Arts." *Shamanhood and Art*, edited by Elvira Eevr Djaltchinova-Malec, Tako Publishing, 2014, pp. 291–307.

Necipoğlu, Gülru. "From Byzantine Constantinople to Ottoman Kostantiniyye; Creation of a Cosmopolitan Capital and Visual Culture under Sultan Mehmed II." *From Byzantion to Istanbul: 8000 Years of a Capital*. Istanbul: Sakıp Sabancı Museum, 2010, pp. 262–278.

Nikčević, H. "Mere Image: Caravaggio, Virtuosity, and Medusa's Averted Eyes." *Refract: An Open Access Visual Studies Journal*, vol. 3, 2020. http://dx.doi.org/10.5070/R73151222.

Pamuk, Orhan. *The Naive and Sentimental Novelist*. Harvard University Press, 2010.

Pamuk, Orhan. *Benim Adım Kırmızı*. Yapı Kredi Yayınları, 2013.

Papila, Aytül. "Osmanlı İmparatorluğu'nun Batılılaşma Döneminde Resim Sanatının Ortaya Çıkışı ve Osmanlı Kimliğinin Resimsel Anlatımı." *Sanat ve Tasarım Dergisi*, vol. 1, no. 1, 2008, pp. 117–134. https://doi.org/10.18603/std.02349.

Prose, Francine. *Caravaggio: Painter of Miracles*. PerfectBound, 2005.

Puttfarken, Thomas. "Caravaggio and the Representation of Violence." *Art/Uměni*, vol. 55, no. 3, 2007, pp. 183–195. *EBSCOhost*, https://doi.org/10.2478/v10008-007-0006-0.

Renda, Günsel. "Osmanlı'dan Cumhuriyet'e İstanbul'da Batı Tarzında Resim: Yeni Denemeler, Yeni Teknikler." *Antik Çağ'dan XXI. Yüzyıla Büyük İstanbul Tarihi*, 2015, pp. 402–421.

Rodini, Elizabeth. *Gentile Bellini's Portrait of Sultan Mehmed II: Lives and Afterlives of an Iconic Image*. Bloomsbury Publishing, 2020.

Rubins, Maria. *Crossroad of Arts, Crossroad of Cultures: Ecphrasis in Russian and French Poetry*. Palgrave, 2000.

Şahin, Seval. "Tevfik Fikret, Parnasizm, Servet-i Fünun ve Resim ile Şiir İlişkisi." *Biyografya*, vol. 7, 2006, pp. 137–156.

Sarpkaya, Doğuş. "'Sanatla uğraşmanın en güzel yanı kendinizde bilmediğinizi keşfetmek.'" *Litera*, March 19, 2023. https://www.literaedebiyat.com/post/res sam-vasif-in-gizli-asklar-tarihi-murat-gulsoy-soylesi

Schneider, Laurie. "Donatello and Caravaggio: The Iconography of Decapitation." *American Imago*, vol. 33, no. 1, 1976, pp. 76–91. *JSTOR*, http://www.jstor.org/stable/26303021.

Şentürk, Emine. "Susan Vreeland'in Anlatısında Barok Bir İnci: Artemisia, Kendini Yaratan Kadın." *Dokuz Eylül Üniversitesi Edebiyat Fakültesi Dergisi*, vol. 11, no. 1, 2024, pp. 137–159.

Seward, Desmond. *Caravaggio: A Passionate Life*. William Morrow & Company, 1998.

Shaw, Wendy. "Where Did the Women Go?: Female Artists from the Ottoman Empire to the Early Years of the Turkish Republic." *Journal of Women's History*, vol. 23, 2011, pp. 13–37. https://doi.org/10.1353/jowh.2011.0008.

Sohm, Philip. "Caravaggio's Deaths." *The Art Bulletin*, vol. 84, no. 3, 2002, pp. 449–468. *JSTOR*, https://doi.org/10.2307/3177308.

Stutley, Margaret. *Shamanism: An Introduction*. Routledge, 2003.

Tekin, Talat. *Orhon Yazıtları*. Simurg, 1998.

Uysal, Zeynep. "The World of Wonders of the Naïve and the Sentimental Novelist: Constructing Visuality in Orhan Pamuk's Fictional Poetics." *Texts, Contexts, Intertexts*, edited by Julian Rentzsch and Petr Kucera, Ergon Verlag, 2022, pp. 437–452.

Uzundemir, Özlem. "Benim Adım Kırmız'da Doğu ile Batı, Geçmiş ile Günümüz Arasında Diyalog Arayışları." *Doğuş Üniversitesi Dergisi*, vol. 2, no. 1, 2001, pp. 112–119.

Uzundemir, Özlem. *İmgeyi Konuşturmak: İngiliz Yazınında Görsel Sanatlar*. Boğaziçi Üniversitesi Yayınevi, 2010.

Vassaf, Gündüz. *Ressamın İsyanı*. Everest Yayınları, 2023.

Wallis, Robert J. "Art and Shamanism: From Cave Painting to the White Cube." *Religions*, 10, 2019, 54. https://doi.org/10.3390/rel10010054.

Warwick, Genevieve. *Caravaggio: Realism, Rebellion, Reception*. Ed. University of Delaware Press, 2010.

Wisch, Barbara. "Seeing Is Believing: St. Lucy in Text, Image, and Festive Culture." *The Saint between Manuscript and Print: Italy 1400–1600*, edited by Alison K. Frazier. Toronto: CRRS, 2015, pp. 101–141.

Yelda, Vasıf Ekrem. Retrospektif. January 20, 2023. https://muratgulsoy.wordpr ess.com/wp-content/uploads/2023/03/retrospektif-1.pdf

"Yüksel Arslan." *Galeri Nev*, galerinev.art/en/yuksel-arslan. Accessed June 3, 2024.

One Final Note for the Reader

During the publication process of this book, inspired by Gündüz Vassaf's work, I made an unforgettable journey to the island of Sicily, encompassing Syracuse, Messina, Taormina and Catania. Accompanied by my faithful travel mate, my sister Zehra and following in the footsteps of Caravaggio, I had the privilege of observing some of his masterpieces in their original locations; *Burial of St. Lucy* at Santa Lucia al Sepolcro in Syracuse and *The Adoration of the Shepherds* and *The Raising of Lazarus* in the Regional Museum of Messina, which was intellectually stimulating, but also extremely challenging amid intense August heat. Yet, when you are truly drawn to something, it is as if the universe starts aligning itself in subtle, meaningful ways. Standing before *Burial of St. Lucy*, I was immediately struck by how dark the painting truly is. Each time the light flickered on—as the church intermittently illuminates the painting—I realized with a sense of awe that Caravaggio's, Vassaf's and my own arrival in Ortigia, Sicily, albeit years or centuries apart, created a profound connection that went beyond mere coincidence, all bound together by the power of art.

www.ingramcontent.com/pod-product-compliance
Lightning Source LLC
Chambersburg PA
CBHW070913100726
47907CB00008B/2307